THE SECRET

1944, London. A young man is killed in an air raid, leaving a wife, two children and a secret. Ailsa, Margaret and Luke are persuaded by Jaime's brother Cal to return to the North East, to the town he came from. Despite their grief and bitterness, they find a new life there: the children make firm friends with Danny and Shannon Logan, whose father Keir drinks and whose mam, Jessie has a secret of her own. Against their families' better judgement, the young people form a bond which sustains them in hard times, and which will ultimately prove unbreakable...

THE SECRET

THE SECRET

by

Elizabeth Gill

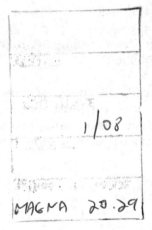

1/08

MAGNA 20.29

Magna Large Print Books
Long Preston, North Yorkshire,
BD23 4ND, England.

British Library Cataloguing in Publication Data.

Gill, Elizabeth
    The secret.

    A catalogue record of this book is
    available from the British Library

    ISBN   978-0-7505-2803-0

First published in Great Britain in 2007
by Severn House Publishers Ltd.

Published in Large Print 2008 by arrangement with
Severn House Publishers

Magna Large Print is an imprint of Library Magna Books Ltd.

Printed and bound in Great Britain by
T.J. (International) Ltd., Cornwall, PL28 8RW

For Helene and Trish with love and thanks

One

London, January 1944

Sometimes they went to a hotel near Charing Cross Station. Jaime thought the afternoons spent in bed there with Nancy were the happiest times of his life. He had loved the big gilt bed and the blue velvet curtains.

Lately she had moved into this flat on the North Side of the Common across from where he lived with his wife and two children. He hadn't wanted her so close. He did not like to think there was nothing between them but a big piece of grass.

He would lie awake at night with Ailsa breathing beside him and think of Nancy alone in her bed a short walk away. She liked the danger of it. He thought that laughable. His wife would not think in a hundred years that he could be having an affair.

He worked for the government, the Ministry of War Transport, a leg injury which left him with a limp had kept him out of the forces. He made a lot of money and he enjoyed spending it, mostly on the black market, and they rented a large Victorian house with spacious rooms.

Now he watched Nancy lying still, her eyes closed, her hair falling over one cheek, her arm flung across the pillow. Her skin was so white, so pretty.

The air-raid siren had gone long since but not the all-clear. He no longer cared. They had made love after the siren and since then Nancy had gone to sleep, she cared so little either.

She had asked him several times to leave his wife and children for her and since he had not done so she had ceased to question him.

He had been with her since half past four. It was his favourite time of the day. When he had been a little boy the chink of teacups and the smell of coffee cake and the fire in the dining room at home had been everything he had wanted.

Even now he felt homesick for Northumberland but it was not for something that was real any longer, it was for the time when he had thought that happiness was lasting.

He heard Nancy say his name and turned further over towards her. She was as unlike his wife as she could be. Maybe that was the point. She was not the mother of his children, waiting at home for him.

He hated how Ailsa was always waiting. He did a job he didn't like to provide for his wife and children and it was a good job and he was good at it but it had never been what he wanted. He felt as though his life had been a complete waste.

Ailsa was a pale thin shadow of the lovely blonde girl he had married. She took solace in her children and her piano, which he had learned to hate the sound of, and he had gone to other women.

Until Nancy. Their affair had been going on for two years. Several times he had almost left Ailsa. He didn't know what had stopped him, it was certainly not the children.

He had been fond of them when they were little but they were fourteen, twins, Margaret and Luke. There had been no more children, the horror of having them had put Ailsa off sex for good. She had spent a good deal of time crying after they were born and had told him to sleep elsewhere, so he had.

He supposed the twins were like all people their age, half-formed, rude, boisterous, dull and expensive. They were to educate, feed, clothe, house and nothing was enough for them.

13

They were always wanting things and they whined continually. Margaret had dull brown hair, had to wear glasses over her short-sighted eyes and was overweight. Luke looked like his mother and was almost unbearably handsome, with pale blond hair, skin that browned golden given a day of summer sunshine and exquisite blue eyes with long dark lashes.

He was tall and slender, elegant and intelligent. Jaime had brought him up to rough games and he took those in his stride too. Somehow Jaime could not forgive his son that he was apparently perfect.

Perfection was boring but so too was the daughter, who was not very bright. She did badly at school, she couldn't sew, she couldn't make a cake without burning it. Margaret had no shining qualities whatsoever and she was most unattractive. She was quiet almost to the point of being taciturn and cared nothing for the things most girls loved, pretty clothes, dancing classes.

Thinking of the children made him even more reluctant to go home. There was nothing to get him through the evening's dullness other than a particularly fine bottle of Scotch he had been wading his way through. It took the edge off his boredom.

Ailsa didn't drink. She was too good to have any faults.

Nancy had lots of faults, it was one of the reasons he loved her. She swore and drank and cared nothing for what people thought and she accepted him as he was, she wasn't always wishing he wouldn't drink so much or that he would come home sooner or that he would pay more attention to the children. This was his favourite place to be, safe against the warmth of her soft body.

Luke and Margaret took the dog, Roly, out.

'Don't be long,' their mother called from the house, 'it's getting dark and it's going to rain.'

She had made a carrot cake, Luke could smell it, a proper cake with margarine and sugar. Today was a special day, it was their parents' wedding anniversary and later there would be dinner, his mother had been hoarding ingredients. Wouldn't their father be surprised and pleased, she said, their sixteenth anniversary? She hoped he wouldn't be too late.

'He's always late,' Margaret said as they left the house, Roly bounding as far ahead as his lead would allow.

'He has a difficult and important job,'

Luke said. He was very proud of his father.

They walked across the Common, munching the Maltesers which their sweet ration allowed them, slowly because the taste of the chocolate was so special. Not far away was an old church, dark in the growing shadows, several pubs and houses, some of which had been bombed ages ago and had boarded-up windows and mended doors.

Their mother had been right, it began to rain when they were too far to get back without being soaked. He could hear Margaret swearing under her breath as they turned around. Great big drops began to fall. The air-raid siren went. Margaret gathered Roly's lead close and they ran for home.

The rain stopped almost immediately. Out of breath, Luke was aware of a strange silence and then, seemingly from nowhere, there was an almighty explosion as though from every part of the Common, the sound of glass breaking and the suck and pull of buildings blowing up. They drew back and Margaret gathered both him and Roly in and they tried to make themselves as small as possible.

Luke had no idea how long they huddled there, only that there was eventually an all-clear. His sole thought was to get back.

As they drew closer wardens appeared on the North Side of the Common, blowing whistles, and he could see that part of the street had been completely ruined. Not their house, please God not theirs, but the South Side appeared to be unharmed, no noise came from there, no smoke. He and Margaret ran with the dog, not looking at one another.

And then they saw their mother running down the street to them. Luke was so relieved, so pleased that he wanted to cry. She gathered them both to her and the dog.

'Thank God you're all right,' she said, 'I was so worried about you,' and she kissed Roly on top of his head.

Jaime did not come home. This was not unusual and she had often telephoned his work to find out where he was and been embarrassed because he had already left.

He had forgotten their anniversary. She should have been used to it by now, she thought, but she had reminded him when he left that morning, so she would have thought he could keep the information inside his head for the rest of the day. He had gone without her seeing him and she had been upstairs and called down as he left, 'Don't forget, I'm making a special meal tonight for our anniversary.'

'I'll be back on time,' he said and clashed the outside door.

She gave the children their meal and waited. After they went to bed – but not to sleep, she could hear them talking upstairs – there was a knock on the door and she opened it to find a warden, looking apologetic, concerned.

'Mrs Gray?'

'Yes.'

'Would you be able to come along with me, please?'

She hesitated. She didn't like to leave the children but then Evie, their general maid and housekeeper, was in.

'Why?'

'We think your husband may have been hurt.'

She went upstairs and knocked on Evie's door and when it was answered told her and then she collected her coat and went back downstairs. Luke and Margaret came out of Margaret's room and on to the landing.

'Where are you going?' Luke asked.

'I'll only be a few minutes.'

'I'll come with you,' he offered, already

turning around in his striped pyjamas, ready to go and dress. Ailsa shivered. It wasn't warm up there.

'No, you stay here and look after Evie and Margaret.' It was best to appeal to his instincts, she thought. 'I won't be long.'

Very often Luke disobeyed her but he didn't now and stood there, shivering with cold and perhaps with fright like the child he thought he wasn't.

Margaret looked like a ghost in her long white nightdress, her hair plaited so that it would not tangle while she slept. Her hair was her only claim to beauty and of late she had wanted to cut it. Ailsa felt such love for them that she didn't want to go.

'I won't be long,' she promised and stumbled back down the stairs.

She clashed the door and then followed the warden across the Common through the darkness. It was bitterly cold now.

Part of the street had been completely ruined and he preceded her to a house which no longer had a front door. The back of the house appeared to remain, the steps were badly damaged but part of the front wall was still there. All around there were mountains of rubble.

Worse still, in the shadows there were two

bodies, covered up and not yet taken away. Perhaps many people had died and they had just been found. The warden uncovered one of the bodies and shone a light.

'Is that your husband, Mrs Gray?'

Ailsa made herself look though there was nothing to look at, just a corpse where a person had once been, the face of her husband but nothing to do with him somehow.

'Yes.' Then her gaze strayed to the other. 'Who is that?'

'I don't know.'

Another warden from further across did not even look up. He said, 'Nancy Carpenter.'

The warden near her did not look at Ailsa.

They had been listening for her, she thought as she made her way back to the house, trying to imagine what she would tell them. She didn't know which had been the greater shock, finding Jaime dead or the realization that he had been with another woman, had possibly died in her arms. There were worse ways to go, Ailsa thought bitterly.

She walked back, trying to put off that she had to tell the children their father was dead. It had never been such a short walk home. She went in as softly as she could but they had been waiting, listening and the moment she was safe in the hall the sitting-room door opened and there they stood, Evie behind them, the two children in their dressing gowns and slippers, their faces already half expecting what she had to tell them.

Ailsa didn't know how to say it.

'It's Daddy, isn't it?' Margaret said, and when they waited she said into the silence,

'Yes. He was ... he had to visit several houses in the area today and...' She was not good at lying, she knew.

She didn't look at them as she stumbled but they would think that was shock and they would be too shocked to notice that she was making a mess of this. They must never know. It was important not to spoil their memories of their father.

Margaret began to cry. Luke stood, white-faced for a few seconds and then bolted. Evie took Margaret into her arms. Luke came back and stood on the landing for a little while after they had gone downstairs, she could see him through the banister rails. Then he must have remembered that he was meant to be grown up and he came down the stairs and looked his mother in the eyes and said,

'Is there anything I can do?'

Two

Northumberland, January 1944

Callum Gray stood by the window of the small morning room in the old vicarage. He could see right across the gardens and since the garden belonging to the church here had been made over to growing vegetables he thought of how it had once been, elegant lawns and rose beds, and how when he was a child his parents would bring him here on sunny afternoons.

He would play with the vicarage children and they would drink tea and eat scones on the lawns. He remembered the long sweeping staircase, the huge upstairs rooms which overlooked the fields that led to the beach and the elegance of the downstairs rooms well looked after by servants.

It was a different world now. The house was no longer lived in by the vicar, he had a much smaller house near the church. This one had been bought by a retired businessman and his wife, they had come to the country after he had made a lot of money and been able to give up work young and they had been here since before the war began. Two of their three children had died in this war. The third, a young woman, hovered in the doorway now, saying awkwardly, 'How lovely to see you, Cal,' and then she closed the door.

He turned and looked at her. 'I was just admiring the garden.'

'There isn't much to admire any more,' she said. 'What can you grow in January? But I have lots of plans. As soon as the weather gets better–'

'Phoebe...' He stopped there. Having interrupted her he couldn't go on.

'There's something wrong, isn't there?' she said.

Phoebe, Cal thought, always assumed there was something wrong. Why should she not? Both of her brothers had been fliers, both had been shot down. She was used to tragedy, as were so many people, and her parents were in mourning for their sons.

He remembered her in 1938. She had been beautiful, always laughing. Life had defeated the family and she was trying, desperately and alone, to bring back some sort of normality.

Her father was always busy gardening, out

24

helping people, doing what he could to keep the grief at bay with activity. Her mother, Cal thought, had long since given up and spent the dark winter afternoons with sewing in her hands by the fire.

The vicarage was a huge freezing pile and they had no help, all the able-bodied people being involved in war work. This room had been dusted recently but its fire was almost out and as he spoke he could see his breath.

When he didn't answer her she said, 'I should have attended to it sooner,' and got down and began to pile little sticks in intricate fashion above the dying embers.

'You don't want to marry me, do you?' Cal said. She looked up and then got up as the flames began to show themselves around the dry sticks.

'You said a week. It's only been six days.'

'How can it take a week? Surely people know instinctively if they want to marry somebody?'

'It's not as simple as that. If I leave my parents who will they have?'

He helped her to her feet.

'It's not as if you're going anywhere. It's the same town.'

'Yes, but…'

He was, he thought, impatient. It was one

of his biggest faults. For years his parents had been telling him to marry and for years he had put it off. He was forty-three and if he didn't marry now, as his father was so fond of telling him, he wouldn't marry at all.

'Jaime will never come back,' his father had said, 'and as for that boy of his...'

Jaime was the prodigal son, the younger one who had got out, had not wanted the business or anything to do with it and when his parents tried to control his life he had left.

The two sides of the family had met on short stilted occasions, always in London since Jaime had sworn never to return to Northumberland.

There was rejoicing when the twins were born but as they grew older they had turned out to be wilful, rude, short on attention, in fact fairly normal, really, he thought. Margaret looked like her father. Luke was exactly like Jaime in character though he looked like his mother and would never make a foundryman, his father had decided. Jaime was inclined to agree. So Cal was left to consider marriage and children.

Phoebe was younger than he was, not thirty-five, though the eldest child. Perhaps that accounted for her feeling of responsibility towards her parents, he thought, but she seemed to like him and he had that age-old stupid desire to try and rescue her as though she were Rapunzel.

She could have done a great many things, the war gave people excuses to leave and go to new experiences, but Phoebe could not because her brothers had died. She was caught here, in the huge vast coldness of the vicarage and her parents' memories.

She looked pale with tiredness, he thought now, struggling to keep things going, to be cheerful for her parents, to bring in the wood and coal, to clean and cook and even shoot. Stupidly, that was what they did together. They went shooting on Saturday and Sunday afternoons, amidst the cold wet trees, down in the wood below the small town.

He didn't think her father approved of such things on Sundays – he was a devout man, helping at the church was one of his main activities – but Cal didn't have a lot of time and teaching Phoebe to shoot had been one of the few pleasures of the war.

She handled a shotgun better than most, he thought with satisfaction, and they needed the meat, no matter what it was. Food was scarce and it was part of her pride that she could put on the table rabbit pie or pigeon stew with vegetables she had grown.

Shooting was hardly a romantic pursuit, the dead birds, the noise of the gun, the waiting with the dripping trees sending the wet down your neck, the wishing you had stayed at home as your fingers numbed and the day grew dark.

There was nothing to look forward to any more. The war had been going on for four years. He was beginning to think that it would never end, that things would never be anything but worse.

Phoebe was his only social life and he was hers. She did not venture beyond the vicarage gardens without a good reason. She was indeed imprisoned there by her mother's ceaseless polite demands and her father's worried face. If they could not find her they assumed something had happened.

'Phoebe...' He got hold of her. He had never done such a thing before unless it was to steady her beyond a rabbit hole when she stumbled. 'I'll find help for your parents. I want you to come and live with me.'

She looked hopefully at him and then she smiled.

'Kiss me then,' she said to his surprise, and when he did it was delightful. He had forgotten that even in the most difficult

28

times there is always something of joy.

As soon as he had gone Phoebe regretted it. She had changed her mind a dozen times in the last six days. She could not leave her parents and they did not want her to leave but they did want her to marry and have a child. Their lives were so empty.

She walked slowly into the sitting room and they both looked up, her mother from her knitting, her father from the small desk in the corner to one side of the fire. They didn't say anything.

'We're to be married,' Phoebe said and she felt like a prison door was shutting.

What else would she do with her life? She was almost thirty-five. She pretended to herself that she looked younger but on bad days the mirror told her differently. If she didn't marry him no doubt she would never have another decent offer and she would live and die in her parents' home. It was not an idea to be borne.

They had tea by the fire and she could see the relief on their faces.

Cal trudged home, more weary than he could think. His first feeling had been one of release, he hadn't known that he had been working up to asking Phoebe to marry him for months and had – yes, he had been putting it off. His parents both looked up now as he walked into the drawing room and he thought they were waiting for him to tell them that he had done what they wanted, so he did and they were pleased.

'Well?' his father prompted.

'She agreed,' Cal said and all the enthusiasm fell away from him. That was what she had done. Phoebe might have affection for him – in fact he was certain of it – but love?

No, she did not love him. She needed rescuing, though she would not have admitted to it, and he was apparently her only way out. Her parents approved of him and his parents liked her. They were both smiling now.

'When is the wedding to be?' his mother said.

'I don't know.'

'You're neither of you getting any younger. You'd best get on with it,' his father said. Cal thought yes, they were desperate for a grandchild, somebody here, somebody they could watch grow up, somebody they could groom to take over and he and Phoebe would have the added pressure of being obliged to have a child as soon as possible.

A wedding during a war without finery, without expense and without stopping the huge amount of work he did.

The telephone shrilled in the hall. He went out and answered it. Ailsa's voice wobbled from the other end. Cal's heart beat hard. There was something the matter. He knew it. He was not going to get through the day easily, whatever had made him think so?

'Cal?'

'Ailsa? Are you all right?'

'No.'

He waited.

'It's Jaime. He's dead.'

All his life somehow Cal had waited to hear it. That he would never see his brother again. It should not have been a loss, Jaime had never liked him, but because they were not close in a way it was even more of a loss.

That kind of thing – you couldn't have what you wanted somehow. People never loved you like you wanted to be loved, but he could remember when they were small children going to a country show and always knowing where Jaime was with an extra instinct. He knew that however far apart they were that day they would always find one another.

That was what had been lost, that flawed regard, the intricate relationship which you could not replicate with another person.

He wanted that day again, seeing Jaime's head in the distance, the way that he had shouted and his brother had turned, laughing, the sunshine, the hills, the horses, the way that the farmers stood about talking in the beer tent, the families with their dogs and their chatter. He had wanted that day to go on and on for ever but it would not, because somehow there was to be no perfection between them.

It was Ailsa's fault somehow. They had both loved her but she had chosen Jaime. He understood. In the same circumstances any woman would have.

Jaime was charming, funny, clever, at home on all social occasions, his very presence guaranteed a shining evening, whereas he was just the older brother, doing the right thing, expected to do so, sure that he did. He carried the weight, the responsibility. He did it again now without wavering but in his heart he wanted Jaime back, he wanted the childhood which was lost.

Three

From the windows on late foggy afternoons, Ailsa watched Luke and his friends, kicking a ball about in the street. Luke was very good at football.

Jaime had been very good too. At one time he had thought his dream would come true and he could play for a top team, for Newcastle or Sunderland. He had never been a golden boy, though, like Luke. Luke seemed not to care or just took enjoyment from the game. If he had any ambition he had not mentioned it.

Margaret did not go outside for days after her father died or see her friends and she had no conversation. She did not speak even at mealtimes, so that Ailsa worried about her.

Ailsa heard the children talking when they were upstairs at night but they did not include her. She did not want to be included, she wanted her life to be how it had been in the first days of their marriage, before he went off and left her with the responsibility of the children and the future.

There was the funeral to be arranged. Ailsa's parents had died, her mother when she was younger and her father since she had left the north to come and live here in London, but Jaime's parents were still alive and they would come with his brother to stay.

Ailsa had not seen them in a long time. It had not occurred to her before now that they were old people. She wished the time back. She did not want Cal and his parents here and for Jaime not to be. She did not want to face the future, she preferred to stay there by the window, watching the children play, pretending to herself that everything was all right and that Jaime would come back as the fog darkened, as the evening fell.

Cal had stayed after the telephone call, glad of the cold in the hall, wondering how he would explain to his parents what had happened. However did you accept the death of a child, no matter how awkward that child had been?

They had never got on with Jaime and he had on several occasions that Cal could remember said he did not like them but it had been a long time ago and he had been young but they would not be able to have that time again to make any repairs to the difficult relationship with their younger son.

Eventually his mother, sensing that there was something wrong, came out of the sitting room. Closing the door she hesitated but she said, 'It's bad news, isn't it?'

'Yes, it is.'

'Come in to the fire, dear. Whatever it is we can stand it. Don't keep it to yourself.'

And that was when Cal remembered that he was the less favoured son. Somehow though they had disliked Jaime they had admired his spirit, his ability to get away, the mystery and joy of him, the elusive quality. They had loved all that.

Now it was gone. He missed Jaime too, he missed the charm, the laughter, the way that they had been little together and played treehouses in the garden, and sneaked across the railway into the football ground on Saturday afternoons, and had gangs.

He followed his mother inside and told them simply that Jaime was dead. They took comfort in one another. His father held his mother's hand and she turned in towards him. That was the first time Cal wished he had married Phoebe before all this happened, so that he would have somebody special to comfort him.

He found Phoebe in the kitchen when he walked back to the vicarage through the blackout. He went to the back door. He did not want to frighten anybody but neither did he want to be formal or to have to explain himself to her parents first so he opened the back door after knocking and swiftly let himself into the room before light should escape. He had been right, Phoebe was washing up at the big white sink. She looked surprised but not displeased to see him.

'Sorry to barge in,' he said. She assured him that it was quite all right and he said without any more ado, 'My brother has been killed by a German bomb.'

'Oh, Cal, how frightful,' she said, wiping her hands on a cloth and coming over to him.

'I thought I had better tell you. I shall have to go to London and help to make what arrangements are necessary. I don't know how long I will be gone.'

She said all the right things. She always did. It was the only comfort. She didn't take him into her arms, they didn't know one another that well. He wished she would, he wished somebody would.

Four

Luke remembered stupid details about the day his father died, that his mother had baked – he could after that not face the smell, one of the most precious of all – and they would have sat by the fire and had tea. Other people went on sitting by the fire and having tea but for them the end of the day could never bring comfort again. He learned to hate five o'clock.

It was the worst night of his life. He missed his father even though he acknowledged that in the past few years they had not seen much of him so that in a way they had always missed him.

It had been several years since Luke had seen either of his grandparents. He barely remembered them. He had the impression that they had not liked his mother though he had no idea why. Their presence was just something more to be faced. Things were as wrong as they could be.

Uncle Callum was very scary, Luke decided, like a larger version of Jaime without the sense of humour, tall and spare, the kind of person who would not put up with any nonsense, Luke thought.

He rarely spoke. He didn't direct any of his remarks to the children but he helped with things. Luke had crept down to the sitting room late at night and heard them talking in low voices about what would be done and how things would be organized, so in a way it was just as well that Callum was there, even though Luke's mother seemed hardly aware of his presence.

At least it stopped Luke from feeling as though he had to behave like a man and take charge of things. The idea of taking charge of anything horrified him. He knew that his mother was completely capable, she had always been so, but since his father's death she had turned into somebody different, vague, absent-minded, shocked.

Luke's grandparents came the day before the funeral. His grandmother was large, red-faced and wore a black coat with a fur collar and a huge hat with a feather. His grandfather was tall and serious looking. They were prosperous people from Northumberland, they owned a steel foundry which made castings for ships.

They had strange accents with flat vowels

which in the few moments he and Margaret were alone they imitated with varying degrees of success. He was just pleased he didn't have to introduce them to any of his friends.

They talked to his mother and not to him – he had taken to listening at doors, sometimes it was the only way you could find out anything – and they urged his mother to go and live with them. His mother made vague noises about friends. Who these were Luke had no idea, he thought she made them up as an excuse not to go but he would have been glad of any excuse. His grandmother, however, wasn't having any of that.

'Friends aren't the same as family and it isn't as though you belong here or have relatives here.'

Luke held his breath, hoping his mother would not be swayed by this. It made him want to run into the room and declare that he had no intention of leaving London, that he didn't want to go to some horrible ugly place in the north. His friends were here, his home. But of course he couldn't say anything, they wouldn't have listened to him anyway and they would have thought him very rude, firstly for listening and then for voicing his opinion in this matter.

'What are you doing?'

He jumped at the sound of Margaret's soft voice in his ear as she joined him on the landing.

'They're talking about us going to live in the north.'

Margaret slid down beside him.

'We can't do that,' she said, which was exactly what he thought.

Mrs Evelyn, who had been their cook, went off to live with her sister in Portsmouth when her sister's husband was killed and it coincided horribly with what had happened to their father, Luke thought – he was torpedoed twice before they finally got him, she said, burned in the sea. He had had terrible scars.

Mrs Evelyn gave them each a shilling before she left. It was instead of hugging them, which she did not feel she could do. Luke thought he would have traded much more than a shilling for her to hug them.

That night Luke couldn't sleep. Margaret cried. He heard her through the wall. He crept into her room in the darkness and heard her draw in her breath and stop crying as he knelt on the bed and then lay down beside her but Margaret ignored him, only saying, 'Go away.'

He wrestled the hot-water bottle from her and took it back to his own bed and lay, looking up into the darkness. He heard his grandparents come to bed but his mother and his uncle were still downstairs, talking, and the thing which was uppermost in his mind became so important that he plunged down the stairs and into the sitting room. They were sitting by the fire and looked up as he opened the door.

'Do we have to go and live with you?' he said.

His uncle looked carefully at him.

'No, you don't have to,' he said, 'it just seemed like the easiest solution. Would you rather stay here?'

'Of course I would,' Luke said and then realized that he was shouting.

Cal said nothing more. Luke waited for him to behave like Jaime did and insist on having his way. Luke had not known until then that he was afraid of his father because Jaime would not have his will put aside for anybody else's needs.

It was the first time he had thought to criticize his father and it seemed a mean-minded thing to do when Jaime was dead. His uncle was obviously quite different.

'You must consider Margaret and your

mother,' was all he said.

'And Roly.'

Cal smiled.

'Roly would like where we live. He could run up the beach every day and chase the gulls.'

'You live by the sea?'

'Don't you remember it? The beaches are being opened up again.'

'I was very little the last time we were there, wasn't I?'

'Yes, you were. You and your mother and Margaret must talk about it by yourselves and not be influenced by what your grandparents or I think. You have to do what's best for you as a family but you're welcome to come and stay with us if you want. You don't have to decide, of course, you could just stay here until you change your minds.'

Luke looked at his mother. She did not have many friends, she had given all her time to her children, and he thought that his father did not like her to have friends, he was possessive of her. Was that love? But then his father had not often been there and Luke was inclined to think his mother must have been lonely. Would she be more lonely if they stayed in London than if she went north?

'Have you a big enough house for us?'

That was apparently funny though his uncle did not laugh. His mother smiled.

'It's a very big house,' she said.

'You have a lot of money, then?'

'Luke—'

'No, it's fair enough. We have a dozen bedrooms, a big garden. We run the steelworks there—'

'I know. My dad told me. He didn't like it.'

'He wanted to do something else.'

'I don't know that I shall ever want to leave here. It's my home,' Luke said. Since nobody argued with him he felt as though he had said sufficient to state his point of view and he went back to bed.

After the funeral Ailsa stood by the sitting-room window, alone for the first time and about to let the tears fall, when she heard a noise behind her. Callum was closing the door behind him, shutting everyone else out.

'Have you come to any decisions yet?' he said.

Ailsa didn't want to talk to him. He had asked her to marry him at one time. It was almost twenty years ago, she thought with a jolt.

She had been eighteen and he had been two years out of university, about to join his father in the business after coming back from working in the south, and the catch of the area. She had refused because she was already in love with Jaime's charming ways.

Shortly after that she had left and they had met briefly at family funerals and weddings and she had no idea what kind of man he had become and she was wary of any man, so it was very difficult now to think of anything to say to him.

'No. I have to consider the children. As you will have gathered they don't want to leave.'

'My father and mother are determined you should come and live with us.'

She turned around and he was smiling slightly, that was a surprise.

'If you do decide to come back to Blackhills with the children we'll be glad to have you. Don't worry about my parents, they're just upset. He was always the favourite, you know, the younger one and funny and… But if you want to stay here I'll be glad to help in any way that I can.'

'That's very kind.'

'Not at all.' Had he always been so formal, so polite? 'I'm sure you have lots of friends in London and the children must have too. It's difficult to uproot children of that age, I should imagine.'

'It's very dangerous here. These last few weeks have been as bad as the Blitz. My instincts are to get out but Jaime wouldn't have the children leave before when things were much worse, so...'

'Perhaps you shouldn't make decisions just yet. I read somewhere that people who are widowed should put off deciding anything. Mind you, you can't make a wrong decision here because anything you do decide can be reversed.'

And that was the difference between the two men, she thought. Callum was the businessman, he calculated everything. Jaime was the dreamer, who calculated nothing except perhaps how to bed his next conquest.

When Callum and his parents had left for the north she tried to talk to the children about moving. She pointed out to them that many of their friends had left the capital long since.

'Some of them left and came back, they hated other places so much,' Luke said.

'If you hate it there we can come back,' she said, 'but I want us to try it, just for a little while.'

'I don't want to go. The north sounds horrible, cold, wet and dirty, and we would have to live with Uncle Cal and Grandmother and Grandfather and I don't like any of them,' Luke said in a burst of candour.

His mother looked sympathetically at him. 'It's too dangerous to stay here, Luke,' she said.

'I don't want to go either,' Margaret said. 'We won't understand a word of what's being said and whatever will we do there?'

Ailsa hesitated. 'We can't afford to stay here, we have very little money and therefore very little choice,' she said. She didn't tell them that Cal had offered to finance her, it didn't seem right that he should do so because his brother had spent all his money on other women and pleasures. She decided to discuss it with them no more but to contact Cal and tell him of her decision and to pack up the house and go.

There was however a great deal to do before then and one of the most difficult jobs was to sort through Jaime's possessions. She left the desk in the study until last because he did not work there, she did not think he had ever worked there, yet it was stuffed with old photographs, letters, diaries.

She had not known him ever to write a diary, yet the one she did find gave her a fascinating afternoon while the children were out. But in the end she wished that she had not discovered it.

It was an old diary from before they were married, when he was young, and it was so obviously not meant for anyone else's eyes. Why had he not destroyed it and was it a sign of Jaime's conceit that he did not choose to hide or get rid of it as she would have done?

She wished her curiosity had not been satisfied, she called herself names afterwards. So much for poking your nose into what was none of your business. She was devastated.

The diary was all about Jessie Logan, a common girl from Blackhills. She had been Jessie O'Brien then and he had loved her.

Ailsa thought how strange and rather twisted it was to envy a woman a man who was dead, a woman who was almost forty and had several children as far as she knew, who was married to a drunk, poor, whom life had treated as badly if not worse than she had been treated herself.

Jessie had had Jaime's love such as Ailsa never had, she could tell by his outpourings.

Even worse there had been a child and though Jessie had denied it he had been convinced that the child, a boy, was his. The worst thing of all was that Ailsa and Jaime had been married shortly afterwards. Had he found out that Jessie didn't want him and married another girl to spite her? And what about the child? Had he known then?

Ailsa could concentrate on nothing but this for several days afterwards. She almost changed her mind about going back to Northumberland because of it but then she thought nobody knew, Jaime was dead. What did it matter?

She felt that she was becoming more and more isolated. She must leave here and carry the secret with her. She put the diary on the fire, page by page, one afternoon so that nobody else would learn the truth if it were so. It was over, finished, dead and buried just like her faithless husband and she would have the strength to begin her life again.

Five

The train was about to steam out of King's Cross Station. Luke wished very much that the people sitting next to the window would let him look out but they seemed deaf and blind to the way that he craned his neck. His mother complained that he should sit still.

The train finally set off but it took a long time to get there and the countryside was dull. He fell asleep and Margaret had to jostle his elbow as the train pulled into Newcastle station. They had to get on another train and had a long wait.

Luke was beginning to think he would be travelling for the rest of his life. They had set off in the morning and it was now mid-afternoon. Finally they reached their destination when it was dusk and unless his ears had given up they were near the sea. He could hear the waves crashing on to the shore.

His Uncle Callum was there to meet them in a big silver Bentley. Luke couldn't help being impressed. It was wartime, most people didn't have petrol for cars, so how important must his uncle be?

Blackhills was not a big town but it was a shock. He had not thought people such as they could live in such an ugly place. There were streets and streets of tiny dark houses and unmade back lanes.

Poorly clad children played and they had dirty faces and straggly hair. It was cold but they wore no coats. There were pit heaps, black mountains seemingly everywhere, and pitwheels.

The house stood on the edge of the town, alone and was big square stone with its own driveway surrounded by trees.

They dragged their suitcases down the side of the house and around to the front door. There were gardens and a porch with stained glass in the door. He thought it looked so welcoming.

The house had gardens all around it and carriage houses which had been turned into garages, a yard at the back with henhouse, washhouse and stables, gardens and fields.

He was given a room all to himself, one of several off a long narrow landing which stretched to either side at the top of the dog-leg staircase and right around in the square of the house. He slept all night from exhaustion but when he awoke it was light and he got out of bed and went to the window.

It looked over the porch at the front of the house and below was the bottom of the gardens, lawns which stretched away almost as far as he could see, rose beds, greenhouses, a wall at the side which divided the front from the kitchen garden, flowerbeds and trees in front of another wall. Beyond it was a paddock, fields to either side, the railway line and what looked to him very much like a football field.

Further over there was a field behind the house and a pit heap and the churchyard. Beneath the football field were houses.

He went downstairs to breakfast and afterwards outside to explore and he took Roly with him. The dog barked with excitement. Luke had been right about the sea. It was not far away, through some houses at the back and across the road.

It was spectacular, he decided, a long wide beach where the waves were making a splendid show. He wished he had asked Margaret to come with him. The beach was empty but for one old man walking his dog and the wind whipped up the waves into white froth.

It was much colder than it had been in

London, even though it was April. Spring must come much later in the north. A bitter wind was blowing across the seafront.

He went back in time for dinner at midday when his grandfather and uncle came in from work. Luke was eager to ask questions but his grandparents seemed to prefer their meals in quiet.

It was Monday and they were having mince with potatoes and carrots. His grandmother's cook was not as good as Mrs Evelyn. His grandmother told him that if he didn't eat it he would get it for his tea, he was lucky to have such good food when there was a war on, and the idea of mince and soggy carrots cold enabled Luke to get the mixture to his mouth until the plate was more or less empty.

That Saturday there was a football match and friends of his grandmother and grandfather came to the house and stood at the upstairs windows with mugs of hot Bovril to watch the game.

The local team were called the Wanderers and played in black and white, the same as Newcastle United, and the talk was of the boys who had gone on to play before the war for the top local teams, Newcastle and Sunderland, and how when it was all over football would resume as normal.

Luke loved football. There were, he thought, some good players among them, it was an exciting match. The Wanderers won, three goals to two and Luke saw them all. It was heaven.

The following day they went, with his grandmother, to the local parish church, down a long wet muddy lane not far from the sea. His grandmother was late but walked all the way down the church to the front.

Luke wished he could hide. Margaret mouthed the words to the hymns. He listened to his grandmother singing loudly. She had quite a good voice for an old lady, he thought, but it was embarrassing to have to listen to it.

Afterwards there was a big Sunday dinner and later he escaped. He walked away from the house. He could hear the sounds of boys shouting. He went past the Mechanics' Institute and there they were, playing football on a Sunday afternoon, such as surely they should not have been.

He did not go too close. He did not understand their conversation, he knew that he spoke differently and that it was unlikely they would let him join in, but his feet itched to be in contact with the ball and in the end he found himself hovering. He was rather afraid that they would attack him for being somebody they did not know.

Eventually a boy kicked the ball between two piles of jerseys which were the goalposts at one end and then he came over. He was dark eyed with straight black hair, worn clothes and the kind of expression which made Luke wonder whether he ought to back off.

'We're one short. Do you want to play?'

Luke nodded.

'Right. There's me and Tig and Spider and Nev. You're marking Lofty.'

Luke was instantly at home there and he had no difficulty in taking the ball from Lofty and depositing it quite easily between the jerseys. By the time he had dribbled the ball three times past hapless feet the other team were calling one another names, shouting, 'Howay, man, Lofty, what yer doin'?' and such like.

From his side there was nothing but silence.

And then he heard a girl's voice shouting from the far end of the lane.

'Come on, our Danny, me mam says yer tea's ready,' and the tall dark boy who had invited him to play stopped.

It was the end of the game. Danny came across.

'You want to play tomorrow?' he said.

Luke nodded, surprised at how friendly the boy was, but he could not help looking at the girl. She had red-brown hair which was like knotted pennies, all the way down to her waist, and huge brown eyes and a sprinkling of freckles. She did not return his gaze. Having collected Danny she went off with him down the main street and was lost to sight.

'Can I come home with you?' he asked Danny the following day, eager to catch another glimpse of the beautiful girl.

'Don't you live at the big house?'

'Can I?'

Danny didn't seem overly keen. Luke thought it was because he didn't like him much, until they got there. Then he altered his ideas. It was a walk away from the village and there were a set of houses above the cliffs, standing quite alone. Luke knew that lots of people were poor but here it was very bad.

The outhouses were falling down, there was rubbish lying about. They went up the back yard in the almost darkness and into the house. It was scrubbed clean, a fire burned brightly in the kitchen grate and there was an appetizing smell of stew.

Three small children screamed and shouted, one of them in an old pram, just a baby, lifting its arms, legs and voice. On the walls were pictures of Mary and Jesus in various unlikely states of grace with hands uplifted in prayer and haloes around their heads and Jesus was being crucified on a statue in the corner.

The girl, to Luke's disappointment, was not there. He did not stay long. Danny offered neither apology nor explanation.

Six

Callum's parents had obviously been talking again about his marriage and Cal had had to go over to the vicarage to see Phoebe's father about the wedding. Had Jaime not left things would have been different, he could not help reflecting.

Cal knew that his father's concern was that he had no son, nobody to carry on the business, and indeed, after Ailsa brought the children home, their grandfather was not pleased with either of them.

'They have just lost their father,' Cal had said, trying to mend things.

His own father looked askance at him across the desk. They were at work and his father had been retired before the war. Now he came into work most days.

Cal wished he would not but there was little you could do. On good days his father showed signs of the brilliance which had enabled him to build this business and on bad days his arithmetic was still better than everybody else's. They had separate offices and tried not to interfere in one another's jobs but it was not easy.

'Margaret must be the plainest girl in the world and as for Luke … he'll never make a foundryman, it ought to be obvious to somebody like you. He's like Jaime was.'

Oh dear, Cal thought, the greatest condemnation in the world was to be 'like Jaime'. Jaime and his father had never got on and Jaime had suffered from being the younger brother and compared unfavourably to Callum so of course as brothers they had hated one another.

Cal disliked being held up as a good example and Jaime did everything he could to be different. In fact Jaime had been brighter than he was, Cal thought now, but nobody could see it and because Jaime's hopes of becoming a footballer were dashed with an injury it took all the spark from him and most of the ambition, though he had held a very responsible post in London. Sometimes when his father was talking disparagingly about him, Cal reminded him of it.

Cal regretted that they had not learned to like one another better, he missed that they might have been older men together and more sensible, might even have mixed socially.

And he missed him on a different level too, the memories of being boys together, fighting and shouting and laughing and plodging in streams and sitting up in bed in the dark, united against the world for all their differences. He missed the childhood friend that Jaime had been, the cricket games and the football and the long cool autumn evenings before their mother called them in for bed.

His father was right, though, Jaime would never have made a foundry manager and Luke was exactly like him.

Now Phoebe's father stood by the meagre fire in his drawing room and looked into it and he said, 'You cannot marry Phoebe after what has happened,' sounding half apologetic.

'We planned it to be soon.'

Mr Wilson gave up watching the fire. His watery blue eyes gave him a tired look as he turned to Cal.

'Not while you are in mourning for your brother, though, surely,' he said.

Cal wanted to say that he wasn't in mourning and it was only then that he knew he had denied to himself that his brother was a loss. They had barely seen one another for years but in a way this man was right, and the respectability of the situation was not their only concern.

'It's wartime,' he said, hoping to gain something.

'A year, Cal, not less than a year,' and with that Cal had to be satisfied.

When Cal had gone into the other room to make small talk with her mother that chilly evening, Phoebe's father called her into the drawing room to discuss the matter and told her the same thing. She said nothing.

'I'm sorry,' Cal said, when she walked him to the bottom of the drive.

'There's no hurry, surely.'

The trouble was, Cal admitted to himself, that he wished he could marry right away, preferably this minute. His life was so turned upside down with his brother's widow and his brother's children and he had so much to cope with, he was beginning to wish he could have something all of his own, somebody of his own, to talk to late at night in the darkness, to hold. He had felt increasingly lonely since they had come back, he wasn't quite sure why but there was no going against her parents' wishes. He would have to be patient and wait.

Seven

It was mid-evening. Danny sat at the window upstairs. It was cold in the bedroom but it was his only chance of solitude. From downstairs he could hear Shannon's voice and his mother's. The children were playing in the back street and any minute now his mother was going to shout up the stairs, 'Our Danny, go and get your dad out the pub,' and he would be swallowed up into the night. He would make his way through the darkness to the pub on the front. If his dad had not frequented it he thought he would have liked the building even so.

It stood on the edge of the sand like it was trying to hold back the tide single-handed. Always at this time of year part of it, usually its back door, would be washed into the sea in the spring tides.

Danny had spent such a lot of time trying to persuade his father home that he should have resented it, only he didn't.

When he was a little kid his dad would carry him home on his shoulders. Now he was nearly as big as his dad. He would push his way in and the men, he knew them all, fishermen, pitmen, steelworkers, would greet him by name.

His dad was a talker, he told stories, and was a good listener too. His family had left Londonderry many years ago, before he was born. It scared Danny how much he loved his dad. He was a big man but he was kind, generous. That was why he never had any money. The whole world was his friend. Everybody liked his dad. He just forgot to come home and almost every night Danny went and collected him. He was glad to do so.

It couldn't even be argued that his father had fair-weather friends who only cared about him when he had money, because his father's friends bought him drink after drink when he had no money, and often he didn't because Shannon or Danny would take from his pockets when he was in bed, sneaking into the room and finding his trousers on the floor.

Danny knew why the men liked his father so much. It was because he was like a candle in a dark room. He was always entertaining. He never got angry or upset with what the world was doing to him.

Maybe he knew he had caused his own problems. Whatever, his dad was interesting to be with even though he had an unreliable temper, and people loved it. When he came back into the house he lit that too. His dad was like a shooting star, everywhere he went he spread light.

His mother went down the back yard now and called the bairns in from the lane. She would put them to bed soon. He got up and went downstairs as she came back inside.

'Precious heart,' his mam said as he set off and she kissed him. She was always kissing him and if he tried to dodge out of the way she would do it twice, so he endured it before leaving the house, pushing his hands into his trouser pockets against the cold and making his way along the front where a bitter wind had flecked the waves with white.

It made Danny think of the most magical evening of his life, when he had been little and his dad put him up on to his shoulders and stepped into the cold sand and there, with the waves fanning out the whole length of the beach like pigeons' wings, he sang, 'O Danny boy, the pipes, the pipes are calling…'

His father had a fine and melodious voice

and Danny was certain that all the angels in heaven were listening to him. The darkness came down, the moon floated above the water like a pearl, the sky cleared, the stars twinkled and his dad ran in and out of the waves with Danny on his shoulders and then up and down the sand while Danny shrieked with glee.

He pushed through the men but when he got to the bar the landlord saw him and said to the tall man nearby, 'Keir, your lad's here.'

Danny, regrettably, liked the pub as much as his dad did. They were all drunk by then. It happened the same every night and Danny loved it, his dad would greet him as though they hadn't met in weeks and would tell him how glad he was to see him. His dad's friends all agreed that he was the best lad in the world and Keir was lucky to have him and then his dad would put a hand on his shoulder and they would walk home. It was Danny's favourite time of day.

'Who is that?'

Why, Margaret wondered, did nobody even introduce her or tell her who anybody was? These people had no manners and also they still thought of her as a child. The woman in the drawing room was younger than everybody else, plain, skinny, pale and very talkative in a nervous kind of way, and kept shooting uncertain smiles across the room at Margaret as though they knew one another.

Her grandmother looked at her in surprise. 'I thought you knew,' she said, 'that's Phoebe Wilson, the young woman your Uncle Callum is going to marry.'

Margaret stared. There was something about Miss Wilson which distinguished her from the women around her and it was because she was not married.

Whatever did she want to marry Uncle Cal for and why did he like her? She wasn't pretty like Margaret's mother and she was awkward in the way that she moved but Margaret regarded her as an ally when she came over and said, 'I'm so sorry to hear about your father. How hard for you to have to leave everything and come here.'

'Are you really going to marry my uncle?'

Miss Wilson's face twisted and she said, 'Yes, but I have no idea when. My father says mourning is not a time for marriage. I'm sure he's right.'

Which left Margaret with the idea that perhaps Miss Wilson wasn't terribly bothered about the whole thing. She didn't blame her. Her uncle was far too old for anybody to want to marry.

Margaret watched Miss Wilson watching her mother and she got the feeling that the two women weren't going to like each other. Was her mother somehow in the way? Another uncomfortable thought occurred to Margaret and when she went to bed that night she sauntered into Luke's room and sat down – he was in bed, reading – and she said, 'Can men marry their brother's widow?'

Luke heard the words. There was a slight pause before he looked up and at her and he said, 'What on earth do you mean?'

'Well,' Margaret let go of her breath, 'could Uncle Callum marry Mother?'

Luke looked at her in astonishment, she could see.

'Why in hell's name would he want to do that?'

'I don't know.'

'And whatever made you think about it? He's supposed to be marrying Miss Wilson.'

'I like her.'

'She seems all right,' said Luke, which was a compliment, Margaret knew.

'You don't think that Mother–'

'She wouldn't want anybody else when she'd been married to Dad. Uncle Callum is worthy and boring, even she must be able to see that. He's the very opposite of Dad so if she did ever think about marrying again it would hardly be anybody like him, would it?' Luke pointed out and Margaret had to be satisfied with that.

Shannon, Danny's sister, heard that Mrs Gray was looking for help in the house. They needed the money very badly so against her mother's wishes – she said she couldn't possibly manage the bairns alone – Shannon trudged into the village and out to the far side, and up to the back door through the yard of the Grays' house.

There were two doors at the back, she wasn't quite sure which one to bang on but then she was answered, ushered into the back kitchen of the house and through a narrow hall and then through the middle door, which led to the front of the house and a wider hall with a glass door at the end and into a big room with a fireplace.

It was a lovely room which overlooked the gardens. Mrs Gray was a large grey-haired old lady and Shannon was rather scared of her but it didn't matter, she didn't have to say much other than 'yes' and 'no' and 'thank you'.

Mrs Gray said she would take her on as long as she was punctual and worked hard. Shannon promised that she would and then went back to tell her mother that she would be going there five days a week to do the cleaning.

Between her and Veronica, their mam had lost two children. Their Theresa was the baby, Mary was four and Veronica was seven. Her mam had often said with sorrow that she had thought her family days were over until Veronica was delivered safely and after that she had two more blessings.

On bad days Shannon didn't regard the children as anything other than a nuisance. How much easier it would have been if there had just been Danny and herself and then she felt guilty and called herself names. She loved the small children, she just wished they weren't to keep.

She felt guilty telling her mother she had got a job because she knew that her mam needed her there, but they needed the money just as much. In fact if she had been twins, Shannon decided, it would have been much better.

Her mam said she was proud of her,

bemoaned the fact as she had done lots of times before that they couldn't afford for Shannon to stay on at school because she was the only one of them any good with learning and books, but they would be glad of the money and she would manage without her. Her mam kissed her and shook her head and Shannon was almost pleased at herself.

When she had left school her teacher had come to the house and told her mam that she was clever and should stay on at school but it had been a dream, nothing else.

Her teacher had offered to lend her books but Shannon couldn't take them. Nothing was safe from the children in their house and she would have been mortified if any harm had come to such precious things. She didn't read any more after she left school. It was like a world with a door closed and she was on the other side of it.

Eight

Margaret became part of her grandmother's sewing circle. She hated sewing and was so bad at it that her grandmother protested. Had she been taught nothing? How long was it going to take her to embroider a few daisies on to a traycloth?

She liked the pretty coloured silks but found herself unable to make her fingers do the required stitches. She was aware of sitting inside on fine afternoons and would have escaped to the beach had she known how to get away. Her grandmother seemed always to be watching her.

Her grandmother could not understand why she wanted to be alone and since she did not know anyone she had no need to leave the house.

To be fair her grandmother arranged for her friends' granddaughters to join the sewing group but Margaret found the conversation invariably about people she did not know. She was homesick for London and after two afternoons spent with the sewing group she ran down the garden, crying.

She stood in a corner beside the lilac tree at the garden wall by the greenhouse, thinking she was hidden from view, only to hear Shannon say behind her, so close that it made her jump, 'Your grandma's looking for you. Something to do with the sewing circle, I think.'

'Pretend you haven't seen me,' Margaret said, sliding up on to the wall and dropping into the long grass which grew in the little field at the other side.

Shannon looked doubtfully at her and said nothing.

They had barely spoken in the days since Shannon had come to clean the house. Margaret had no idea what to say to somebody her own age who was obliged to scrub other people's floors just to get by.

'Where are you going?' Shannon had a soft sing-song voice like balm on cut wounds.

'Anywhere away from here.'

To her surprise Shannon got over the wall and followed her. It was tea time, no doubt she was going home. They crossed the field and reached the railway line.

'I wish I could go back to London,' was all Margaret managed as they climbed the fence and sat on it.

'Your dad died, in the bombing?'

Nobody had mentioned this except Miss Wilson. Margaret had not realized how much she wanted to have somebody say something. Why did people think things were better not talked of?

'He did, yes. I miss him. My mother brought us here. My grandmother wants me to do stupid things and have curly hair. How do you get yours like that?'

'It's natural.'

'Lucky you.'

'I don't like it,' Shannon said with a shake of her head as though it might rid her of the luxuriant brown curls.

They got over the fence and walked up the line, past the pit heap, on to the bridge and gradually made their way along the road which led to the beach.

Margaret had no idea why she preferred the company of this girl who wore hideous cheap flowered dresses and sand shoes because, Margaret suspected, they were all she had.

The other girls she knew seemed insipid by comparison. They played the piano and went to tap-dancing classes. Shannon went home in the evenings and helped to look after her family. She did not have time off.

Margaret went back to the house for tea only to discover that her grandmother 'wanted a word with her'. It was a phrase that made Margaret feel like she was sinking.

'Shannon Logan is not suitable company for you.'

'We were only talking,' Margaret said, gazing out of the drawing-room window at the rockery. Her grandmother's garden was rigid, or was it just that because she didn't like her grandmother much it seemed so? In anybody else's possession it would have been a wonderful garden. It had lawns and big trees and roses.

'I took her on here out of the goodness of my heart but they are hopeless people. Her father is a drunk, I don't know why Callum keeps him on. She is a Catholic and a servant as far as you are concerned—'

'She's not a servant,' Margaret broke in.

Her grandmother looked patiently at her.

'If you persist I shall dismiss her. There are plenty of nice girls from good families. You may spend your free time with them.'

Margaret had no intention of giving up Shannon's company and even less when at the end of the following evening Shannon left and somebody was waiting for her, a tall dark boy in equally shabby clothes.

It was later than usual and Margaret did not get much of a look at him but there was something about the way he turned that made her want to go on watching. He had a kind of grace which she had not seen before, as though he would surround Shannon so that nobody could hurt her.

Margaret called herself silly but the next day she followed Shannon into the back kitchen and asked about him in a teasing way.

'A lad?' Shannon said. 'I don't know who you mean.'

'You met him after work last night.'

Shannon laughed. 'That's just our Danny. He doesn't like me walking home on my own if it's dark when I leave so when he's on the right shift he comes for me. Sometimes he has to get out of bed. I told him he needn't.'

'Why does he have to get out of bed?'

'He's a pitman. He works shifts.'

'My grandma says I'm not to talk to you,' Margaret said, 'but I would like it if we could be friends.'

Shannon looked embarrassed but she was pleased too, Margaret could see.

'You have to mind your grandma,' she said.

'We could meet on your day off.'

'I don't have much time.'

'No, I know you don't,' and Margaret went and left her to her work but later Shannon came to her room, duster in hand for camouflage.

'You shouldn't deceive your grandma but we could talk after I'm finished if you like,' she said.

Shannon was unprepared for Danny's reaction to Margaret. As far as she knew he had never taken an interest in anything other than football. That changed the moment he saw Margaret. Shannon had told him not to meet her but Danny wouldn't be told and as Margaret ran down the path from the side of the house to be with her Danny appeared.

He didn't stare. Danny wasn't given to anything like that, but he did look and Shannon wished she hadn't tried to make friends with Margaret because Margaret was a Protestant and well off and a southerner and talked posh.

As for Margaret, when she saw Danny for the second time she was like a bar of chocolate that had been left too long on the window ledge in the sunshine, Shannon thought.

Shannon could feel the tension between

them even though nobody said anything. Margaret didn't linger, made excuses, backed off and Danny didn't speak all the way home so Shannon said nothing, but it seemed to her she had done neither of them any favours that day.

Danny's instincts were good. During the days that followed he no longer came to the house to collect Shannon but would wait along the road and Margaret was always absent when Shannon left – deliberately so, Shannon thought.

Danny didn't ask about Margaret but then he didn't need to, everybody in the area knew about the two children whose father had been killed in London by a German bomb.

One night when Luke and Danny had been playing football they went to Luke's house, around to the side and up the back stairs. It wasn't at all how Danny had thought rich folk lived. Luke's bedroom when they reached it was as cold as his own and it was a great big place with nobody else in it, he would have hated that. He liked going home and having his sisters sleeping near him. Darkness was bad enough without being by yourself.

What made it worse somehow was that it could have been really nice. There was a big fireplace but the grate was swept clean, a mantelpiece for your important things, a window with shutters which were open and a lot of very big furniture.

Luke produced cigarettes, matches and a bottle of whisky. Danny accepted a glass and a cigarette and sat on the deep window ledge. From there you could see the football field.

Danny watched the door open. Luke turned and his dark-haired sister came softly into the room. She observed the whisky glasses and the cigarettes and then she said, 'Are those Uncle Callum's? You didn't steal them, Luke? If he finds out he will kill you.'

'Oh, shut up,' Luke said mildly.

Danny could feel that she was about to leave. He said, 'Can they hear us downstairs?'

'We're over the dining room so we'll have to be fairly quiet but usually nobody goes in there after tea,' she said.

It was Luke she was watching. Danny willed him to be nice to her so that she wouldn't go. He sensed that she wanted to be there, that she would be alone otherwise.

Shannon talked a lot about Margaret at home, how she had not made friends with anybody else, how well they got on. He could tell that Shannon was proud to be considered Margaret's friend and he could see why.

Luke's instincts were fine-tuned.

'Shut the door or they will hear us,' he said and added swiftly, 'Come and sit down,' in case she thought he wanted her out because Danny was there. 'This is Danny.'

'I know.'

When she hesitated in the middle of the room Luke slid down on to the floor and handed her both his cigarette and his glass. From somewhere he magicked another glass, lit another cigarette.

To Danny's surprise she didn't cough or splutter over the cigarette or the whisky and she regarded him from clear blue eyes behind her glasses.

Danny wondered what it would be like to kiss her. Her mouth was perfectly shaped on the cigarette as she dragged the smoke into her lungs. Her fingers were slender, the nails neat and white on the whisky glass, and her figure was rounded, her skin looked so smooth.

'I wish you'd brought Shannon with you,' she said.

'I will next time. You've done this before,'

Danny guessed.

'All the time in London after Father died,' Luke said. 'Mother didn't notice.'

They talked about football. Danny had the feeling that Margaret didn't mind. He didn't care what they talked about, none of it meant anything. He just wanted to be there with them.

The level on the whisky went down and they were all aware that they could neither laugh too loudly nor make more than very soft conversation. Danny got off the window seat and they sat there on the carpet which covered and warmed the floorboards in the middle of the room.

It was like one of those films, Indians in a tepee sitting about in a circle, and he was aware that it was a magic space and outside of it was their grandparents and their uncle and the pit and Luke's school and the way that her grandmother's house was Margaret's cell.

They were a triangle which could not be invaded. Later, through the sweet whisky haze, he heard the old people come to bed and he envied them their talk, their closeness, how they shut the bedroom door and after that the noise was dulled.

He remembered with glee that it was

Saturday, that he didn't have to get up for work the next day, but he must go home, Shannon would worry, so when the night was cool and old he left Luke and Margaret, thanking them, and made his way carefully down the back stairs.

The stars had never been so big, the sky was lit brilliantly. When he got home Shannon was waiting for him. Everybody else had gone to bed. She looked carefully at him.

'Are you drunk, Danny?'

'I think so.'

'You're turning into my dad.'

'I just went to see Luke and Margaret. Will you come next time?'

'Not if you get drunk. Can you manage the stairs?'

'Of course I can.'

'Quietly then or Mam and Dad will wake up.'

Danny made the bedroom with barely a sound. He wanted to say all sorts of stupid things but he didn't. He was not going to be his dad, Shannon had it wrong, he was going to do wonderful things and get them out of this awful place.

Veronica was sleeping peacefully. Shannon got in on one side and he got in on the other and he thought of Luke sleeping on his own and was sorry for him. The sound of other people's breathing was the most comforting in the world.

Margaret and Luke were surprised to receive a summons to the study the next morning. Usually Callum was too busy to bother with them. He had to keep the works going seven days a week. He didn't look particularly pleased to see them either, Luke noted, as his uncle shot a very straight look across the desk and made them glance at each other sideways.

'I've made arrangements for you to go to school.'

'I thought I was finished with school,' Margaret announced.

'Did you, indeed? I'm afraid not. You'll both go to the local grammar school.'

Luke stared at his uncle's cool blue eyes, somewhat disconcerted to realize they were his own.

'We went to private school in London.'

'Yes, well, there isn't a private school nearby so unless you want to go away to school you'll go to the grammar.'

'It's miles away,' Luke said.

'A mile,' Callum said, 'maybe a little more.

The exercise won't hurt either of you.'

'I'm not going,' Margaret said.

Callum looked at her. Luke was rather glad he hadn't invited such a look. It held tolerant amusement.

'Your grandmother may think embroidering traycloths the limit of your intellectual capabilities. I don't. Women can do almost anything they choose if they have education. Don't you want that?' He gave her time to answer and when she didn't he said, 'You want to be obligated to say to some spotty youth that you'll leave the interesting parts of life to him and stay at home and bake bread?'

'Bread is quite difficult to make,' Margaret said. 'And I think there is slightly more to it than that.'

Callum ignored this.

'Also since you both seem to have sufficient time to sit about with Danny Logan, smoking my cigarettes and drinking my whisky, I think it's best you put at least part of your days to something more constructive.'

There was silence. Luke waited to be told that he was going to be punished or that he was going to be punished if he did it again or to be told that people his age weren't

83

allowed cigarettes and whisky.

'You'll start next Monday. Your mother has agreed to sort out the uniform,' Callum said.

They went slowly upstairs but it wasn't until they reached her room and went in and closed the door that Margaret said, 'Sarcastic bugger.'

Luke sprawled on the bed.

'It could have been worse,' he said.

'It probably will be,' Margaret said.

The summer holidays seemed so short, Luke clung to each moment and yet he didn't want to be there either, he wanted to be in London, not as it was now but as it had been when his father was alive. He could not believe how happy they had been and how unhappy he was here.

The only good times were when he and Margaret and Danny had sat about drinking whisky. It made things improve slightly. His grandparents had altered, or was it just him? Food was scarce and rationed and he was always hungry.

He was out of temper very often though he didn't dare to say much. It was a good thing Danny and Margaret were there because he had almost forgotten what it was like to care about anything.

There was trouble at school almost straight away but he did nothing, just watched the inept scuffling these boys thought was fighting and how the bullies would hold boys down while the others dealt some kind of pain. Because Luke had never challenged anybody they were stupid enough to think he was afraid.

The trouble was that Luke's father had been good at boxing in his youth and from a little boy he had been taught what he called 'the science' of it. Luke had not thought anything about it, he didn't even enjoy it, but when he was younger he would have done anything to please his father. The praise was enough to make him enthusiastic.

Luke knew how to move just out of reach, how to get in under a not very intelligent defence and how to land sparing, effective blows. When he got tired of their bullying he picked the biggest, most offensive of his would-be oppressors and went for him.

By the time the other boy was on the ground Luke was not even out of breath. Everybody else stood well back, astonished looks on their faces while the blood ran down the other boy's face. There would not be any lasting damage, Luke assessed, it was just that it looked bad.

He could not even remember what the dispute had been about. Oh yes, they had tried to take from him the small amount of pocket money he was allowed and he was tired of them pushing him around. Had they rushed him at any point it would have been a different story but they hadn't and didn't.

He got the cane, of course, you always did for fighting, and everybody wanted to be his friend that day. Luke didn't even go back to classes. He took a book and spent most of the day in a little summerhouse he had discovered on the edge of the school grounds. It was out of bounds but he didn't care. What could they do? If they threw him out he would be glad.

By the time he came home the following day his uncle had had a letter and called him into the little study which looked out across the end of the garden where the wall ran between the greenhouses.

'You didn't tell me there was a problem,' he said.

'There isn't,' Luke said, staring past him at the window.

'Fighting. Not attending lessons. Being rude to the teachers.'

Luke was about to be rude to Callum just

to make things worse and then he thought for the first time how tired the man looked. He was out of temper too. Luke was inclined to push him just to see what happened and then it all seemed so terribly unfair that he didn't. Cal didn't want this situation any more than he did.

'I got bullied. They tried to take what little money you and Mother give us. They'd done it several times and I wasn't prepared to put up with it any longer.'

'Good at fighting, are you?' Callum guessed.

'My father taught me.'

'Yes, I thought he must have.'

'You any good?'

Callum seemed surprised at the question. 'Not any more. You do other kinds of fighting by the time you get to my age.'

'I don't like the school but then I don't think I would like any school. I want to leave.'

'Have you thought as to what you would do?'

'No.'

'Would you like to come into the business?'

'No, I don't think so.'

'When you work out what you want to do

let me know. Until then I think you ought to stay at school, don't you?'

'All right,' Luke said, 'but when I want to leave I will leave.'

Callum was too intelligent to argue, Luke thought, or to pretend he was a parent.

'As long as you do something construct-ive, that's fine,' Callum said.

To his surprise also Callum began to make both him and Margaret a proper allowance, paid into their bank, which they could use as they wanted.

'He needn't think I'll like him any better for it, I won't,' Luke declared and then thought how childish he sounded.

Margaret didn't say anything.

'Do you like him?' Luke asked.

'No, of course not. He isn't Daddy and he never will be.'

'I don't think he wants to be, to be fair,' Luke said.

When Luke saw Danny he was ashamed. Luke went to play football but Danny was not there. He went to the house sometimes but Danny was either in bed or at work. A large man turned Luke from the door more than once. Luke saw Shannon every day. Not that she spoke. She was pale and thin and never stopped working.

'When's Danny not at work?' Luke asked finally, in desperation.

'You could come by Sunday afternoon if you want,' Shannon said.

Margaret insisted on going with him. He wouldn't have told her but she overheard Shannon and wouldn't be put off. She didn't say anything when they reached the house though he could have told her it was much better than it had been before. The houses were practically falling down.

Danny opened the door. Their father was nowhere to be seen. He was in bed, sleeping off the pub and his Sunday dinner, Danny said. Their mother had gone to lie down.

They went outside. A cold wind blew down the back lane. It smelled of the sea and it blew the rubbish about and it blew the smell of lavatories towards them.

Sundays were all they had and Luke treasured them. He seemed to spend the rest of the time waiting for Sundays to come round.

He found boxes of cigars in the court cupboard and learned how to smoke those. There seemed also to be an endless supply of whisky. People in business bought them and his grandfather did not drink and did not notice that the bottles disappeared and even though he felt certain his uncle was aware of what he was doing Callum said nothing.

Every Sunday afternoon they went to the beach, taking the children, swimming and sunbathing, and in the evenings when Danny's mother put the children to bed the four of them would go back to the beach and smoke and drink. They would stay out until it was very late and then sneak up the back stairs.

On the fifth Sunday night when they got home the back door was locked and when Luke tried the spare key he carried on him he realized it was bolted. As he turned around he saw his grandfather behind them.

'Where have you been?'

Nobody answered. He ushered them into the house, into the drawing room, where their grandmother, pale-faced, sat waiting.

His grandfather repeated the question. Luke thought there was no point in lying though he wanted to.

'We've been down to the beach.'

'And what have you been doing there, when you should have been in bed?' his grandmother wanted to know. Luke hesitated. 'I can smell alcohol and cigarettes.

How long has this been going on?'

'We did it in London, it's nothing new,' Margaret said. She didn't add 'after our father died' which she could have, Luke thought.

'London ways won't do here,' her grandmother said. 'If you can't behave better than this you will have to go back to London.'

Margaret laughed. 'I wish I could,' she said.

'I know what it is, it's the influence of those Logans,' her grandmother said. 'I shall dismiss that girl in the morning.'

Luke did not realize until that moment that he wanted to run to Callum to save him from what he did. But Callum was away that week on business. It gave Luke a strange jolt. Would his father have helped? Somehow he thought not, but his uncle would, only he wasn't there.

That evening changed everything. Luke would have lied for a month to save Danny and Shannon. He said it was nothing to do with them. He thought afterwards that he said too much. His grandparents were not convinced. The next morning Shannon was turned away at the door. Luke ran after her, touched her arm.

'They caught us coming back last night,' he said.

She smiled. 'It doesn't matter,' she said.

'The money is important to you.'

'I'll find something else. Don't worry about it, Luke,' she said.

Shannon was not at home long before Danny walked in, too clean for her to think he had done any better.

'You too?' she said. 'I think old Mr Gray has been busy today.'

'Nobody else'll take me on, not with old man Gray putting the evil word about.'

Later Luke came to the house and when he saw Danny he turned around and ran all the way to his grandfather's office and burst in. His grandfather, who was writing at the desk, looked up.

'Please get Danny his job back.'

'I didn't–'

'Please. I will do whatever you wish. He has three small children to feed. I won't see them any more and I won't smoke or drink or be rude or … and I will work hard at school and…'

'You will go back to school and behave properly because it is the right thing to do, not for any other reason,' his grandfather said.

'If you will help Danny–'

'None of us will have anything more to do with the Logans,' his grandfather said.

'If you don't help I won't do anything you say,' Luke found himself shouting, 'I will smoke and drink and do dreadful things and never go back to school. I never wanted to come here in the first place. I hate it and I hate you!'

That night he heard noises from beyond his bedroom door and when he ventured on to the landing his grandmother told him to put on some clothes and run for the doctor. His grandfather had collapsed.

Luke dressed in a matter of seconds and ran through the night. Luckily it was only a few houses away. He banged on the door and the doctor's housekeeper eventually answered.

Minutes later the doctor emerged and followed Luke at a steady pace to the house. He went upstairs. Margaret was hovering on the landing as Luke followed. Luke watched as the doctor went into their grandparents' bedroom and closed the door behind him.

'You don't think he's dead, do you, Margaret?'

Margaret said all the right things but Luke

couldn't leave the landing, as though somehow if he did his grandfather would die. He thought back over how awful he had been, how badly he had behaved, how only a few hours earlier he had argued with his grandfather and pleaded for Danny and Shannon and then shouted.

He sat there for so long that Margaret gave up any pretence of sleep and came and sat with him on the dark draughty landing, until they pushed the curtains aside so that the arch-shaped window which threw what light there was on to the staircase began to grey the deepest shadows. The door opened, the doctor came out and Luke could hear his grandmother crying from within.

Nine

They buried his grandfather on a wet September day in the old churchyard which overlooked the sea. The graves there held a mixture of sailors, pitmen, steelworkers, fishermen and their families.

Luke looked out at the stormy North Sea and thought of all the men who had died in the war. At least his grandfather had died at home and was buried where his family and friends could be near.

Luke looked out over the open grave at his mother as they lowered the coffin into it. Everybody else bowed their heads as the vicar spoke but his mother did not. She looked blankly out to sea.

They went back to the house. The rest of the day was spent being polite to his grandfather's friends and business associates who had come to show their respect and comfort his grandmother.

Luke went in search of his mother and it was only then that he thought, watching her back as she stood by the drawing-room window with a cup and saucer in her hand, that she was different since his dad had died, quieter, thinner, older.

'Why did you and Dad leave here?' Luke said.

She turned around, looking at him in surprise, and to his astonishment she told him what he knew to be the truth.

'Your grandfather wanted him to go into the business. He wanted to be a footballer, he didn't care anything for the foundry. They quarrelled because your grandfather said he couldn't do both well. They employed so many men and a man who owned a company could only concentrate on one thing.

'He got hurt in a fight he was trying to stop between two young labourers, lamed his leg and after that they just couldn't agree on anything somehow.'

'But Uncle Callum ran the business, didn't he?'

She hesitated. 'Not at the time. Cal had a good job, he was working in London for a car company and then your grandfather was taken ill and he had to come home. The business wasn't sufficiently profitable to sell and your grandparents were very upset when your father left like that.'

'I'm glad he left. I shall leave as soon as I can,' Luke said.

Phoebe was watching Cal and Ailsa from across the drawing room when everybody was drinking tea after the funeral. She didn't approach. She didn't think Cal was aware of her presence, even. Ailsa Gray was beautiful, fair, slight, she made other women feel enormous beside her. She had lived in London and had sophisticated manners and gave the impression of being very clever. Phoebe never felt quite so much the country bumpkin as she did when Ailsa was in the room.

She had tried to feel sorry for her because her husband had died but it was difficult to feel sorry for a woman when the man you were engaged to looked down at his sister-in-law with sympathy and smiling understanding.

Phoebe told herself in vain that Ailsa was older than she was but that did not stop her from being that horrible thing – ethereal, all straight shining blonde hair, waiflike looks, and she had elegant clothes. Presumably she had bought them before the war but she looked so good in them. Phoebe had never felt so plain, so unnoticed.

97

Ailsa did not stay in the room to drink her tea, as though she could not bear the presence of other people or their condolences. She went off to the music room and after a short while Cal followed her there. Phoebe went on making small talk and smiling at people until she felt like her face had set as blancmange did.

'Are you all right?' Callum hesitated in the doorway as Ailsa finished her second cup of tea.

'Yes. It was just such a shock so short a time after – after...'

'Yes, I know.'

'Awful for your mother.'

'You know how it feels.'

'Not really,' she said.

Callum hesitated in the doorway. 'No?'

Ailsa didn't reply immediately and then she said, 'It was a very bad marriage.' It was the first time she had said such a thing to anybody and she felt at least a stone lighter. Then she glanced past him at the hall in case anybody had heard. He came inside and closed the door.

She bit her lip so that she wouldn't cry in front of him. They hardly knew one another any more and he had enough problems without her making things worse. 'I didn't mean to say that.'

'Why not?'

'It's nothing to you. And besides, you never liked him.'

'I just assumed you were happy.'

'He was...' she said and then stopped. She could hardly tell him his brother had treated her badly. Maybe by men's standards he hadn't. 'I don't think I was the wife he wanted or the woman he wanted. Maybe he didn't want a wife.'

'Or maybe the reverse was true and he wanted more than one woman?' Callum said and she looked at him, surprised at his perception. She had had no idea that he knew or guessed what his brother was like.

Ailsa looked down into her teacup, wondered whether she could put it on top of the piano without dropping and breaking it and then had to get rid of it, her hands shook so much. She managed to let it down on to the window ledge.

'It was both of us to blame, it didn't work right from the beginning but it was much worse after the twins were born. He didn't like them, was jealous of them and they adored him. Children are so time-consuming and two together... He didn't like that my attention was distracted from him and he didn't help, at least I didn't feel as if he did, and … it was quite hard. The least bit of time he ever gave them they were so grateful for. He once told Margaret that she was ugly and Luke that he was too pretty to be a boy.'

Ailsa couldn't see the view any more, the tears blinded her. Callum came over to the window, she heard rather than saw him, he was just a blur in a dark suit.

'And?' he said.

Ailsa tried to look at him.

'And what?'

'I don't know. I've been waiting weeks for you to tell me or if not me then somebody. You can barely speak his name, you hate him so much.'

'Isn't it enough that he didn't like his children and went with other women?'

'It might be but there's more, isn't there?'

She shook her head. Callum waited.

'Tell me,' he said.

'He was … he was with another woman when he died. He had… I suspect he had spent all afternoon there, in bed with her or – or whatever people do. And it was our wedding anniversary. I had spent the afternoon baking a cake, had saved the ingredients, was determined to make things better.

'Don't you think that was incredibly stupid? What was I doing? After years of him behaving like that? I didn't have a marriage and there I was ... baking a wretched cake and he was ... he was... You can't hate people when they're dead, however much you want to, because you win when they die,' she finished and ran out of the room.

The following day the solicitor, Mr Farquhar, arrived and was closeted with Luke's mother, uncle and grandmother for some time. Luke and Margaret hung about, hoping for a clue as to what was happening. Eventually, as the afternoon grew dark, their grandmother came out with a lace handkerchief to her face and their mother supporting her. Their uncle stayed inside.

Margaret followed her grandmother upstairs later, knocked softly on the bedroom door and, receiving no reply, went in.

'Why, Margaret, dear.' Her grandmother, red-eyed from weeping, seemed pleased to see her.

Margaret went over and sat down on the bed beside her.

'Are you all right, Grandma?' she said.

'It was an old will. He made it years ago. I begged and begged of him to make another.

I told Mr Farquhar that it was not right.'

'What's not right?' Margaret said.

Her grandmother stared down from red-rimmed eyes at the handkerchief.

'Your uncle gets almost everything,' she said. 'I can live in this house for the rest of my life, nothing more.'

'Can't you…' Margaret searched her memory for the right words. 'Can't you contest it?'

'What would be the point? All I have is my family. Callum works hard for us, I can't say to him that things should have been left differently. Your grandfather was only trying to look after me but Callum is … he cares for nothing but the business.'

That was the first time that Margaret realized her grandmother didn't like her uncle.

Later she went into her mother's room. Ailsa had not spoken a word to them that day.

'Did Grandfather leave us anything?' Margaret asked. It sounded so rude but it was obvious her mother was not going to tell them what was happening without somebody asking her.

'He left Luke his pocket watch,' her mother said. Margaret thought for the first time that she was like her mother, who managed to give the single sentence an inflection of resigned bitterness Margaret did not recall having heard before.

'You and I got nothing?'

'No.'

'What will we do?'

'I expect we will carry on as usual. I don't think your uncle is going to put us on the street and I do have what your father left us so we aren't destitute.'

'Was it a lot?'

'It wasn't,' her mother said.

'Daddy didn't leave either Luke or me anything personal, did he?'

'No, but then,' she looked up and in an attempt to be reassuring, Margaret thought, she said, 'he didn't think he would die so young.'

Margaret didn't like to point out the obvious, that there was a war on, that hundreds of thousands of people had died, but then you never thought it would be you, so her father had thought the same, no doubt.

'Is there enough money for us to afford a house of our own?'

'Not unless you want to live in a street, in a little terraced house, and have us all work at very disagreeable jobs like lots of other people do.'

'So Daddy didn't have any money?'

'He may have had a good deal through his hands but there was not much of it left.'

'What did he spend it on?'

'Your education, our day-to-day living.' Her mother wasn't looking at her so it was not the whole truth, Margaret thought. Perhaps it was better not to know the truth sometimes.

Late that night Luke had a horrible dream about his grandfather and, unable to rid his mind of it, stumbled downstairs.

To his surprise, considering the grandfather clock halfway up the stairs, beside the mounted head of a deer, had just struck two, there was a line of light under the study door. Luke hovered in the darkness of the hall but it was eerily quiet and lonely. He pushed open the door.

He was cheered for a moment. The fire burned merrily but it was not his grandmother sitting over it, unable to sleep, it was his uncle, fully dressed with a decanter of whisky at his elbow on a small table. The decanter, square and cut glass, looked inviting in the firelight.

Callum put down the glass he was holding.

'Luke,' he said in surprise.

Luke hesitated but was too afraid to go back out into the darkness.

'I had a nightmare. May I come in?'

'Of course you can come in. Close the door, there's a hell of a draught.'

'May I have some of that?'

Callum looked at him for a second and then got up and took another glass from the silver tray on the sideboard. He poured until the short, stout glass was half full and presented it to Luke.

'Sit down,' he said.

Luke took the glass and sipped gratefully, folding his striped pyjama legs beneath him.

'So what was the nightmare about?' Callum said.

'You don't want to know.'

'You're drinking my whisky. Indulge me.'

'I did this.'

'What?'

'This.' Luke waved the glass at him. 'Not in the dream, I did it really,' and he recounted the tale of him and Margaret drinking and smoking with Shannon and Danny and how his grandfather had been so angry and lost them both their jobs.

'And I promised him I would never do it again, that I would go back to school and do whatever he wanted me to and then I

shouted at him and told him I hated him …
and then he died and – and I did it, and that
was what the dream was about.' Luke had
not realized until then that he was crying.
He pulled a pyjamaed sleeve across his face
in disgust.

'You did it from behaving badly?' Callum
smiled.

'It's not funny!'

'Your grandfather did not die because of
you. That's nonsense, Luke.'

It had never before occurred to Luke that
his uncle's cool cynical voice could be of
comfort.

'It isn't,' he said, crying harder for some
reason. 'I wish I was back in London. I miss
my dad.'

He hadn't meant to say that. Nothing
altered in the room. Callum did not react.
Luke swallowed some more whisky. It was
very good stuff, he recognized, much better
than he was used to. His uncle might not
know much but he certainly knew about
whisky. It was smooth and rich on the tongue
almost like fruit.

'He died because his heart was worn out,
not because of anything you did. Do you
want me to take you back to bed?'

'I'm nearly fifteen.'

'Better finish your whisky, then.'

'This isn't the same whisky you let us drink.'

Callum looked respectfully at him.

'What it is to be a connoisseur at your age.'

'It isn't, though, is it?'

'No, it isn't.'

'Don't you mind us drinking it?' Luke couldn't help but ask.

'Why should I mind?'

'Well...' Luke didn't quite know what to say. 'You buy this stuff especially for you. Who is the other bought for, us?'

'Would you like a little more?'

'No, thank you,' Luke said, rather annoyed that Callum couldn't find it in him to act like any decent parent would and be angry. He had to remind himself that Callum was not a parent and therefore didn't know. 'Didn't you ever want children?'

'Don't you think I have enough to cope with?'

'Aren't you going to marry Phoebe Wilson, then?' It wasn't until he said it that Luke knew how rude this sounded.

Cal looked at him, still amused. 'Do you think I should?'

'I think I shall go back upstairs now,' Luke

said with all the dignity he could summon. He put down his empty glass, walked slowly and was asleep within seconds of getting into his suddenly very warm and comfortable bed.

Danny had not expected to like Margaret Gray so that was the first surprise. He had always imagined that when he did like a girl she would be little and blonde and fragile. There was nothing fragile about Margaret. She drank and smoked and swore. She had large blue eyes, accentuated by the glasses which she wore so that he could not help liking the glasses.

Margaret Gray had the most beautiful blue eyes in the whole world. Also she had, Danny was quite certain, the most perfect figure God had ever given a girl. She went in and out spectacularly in all the right places.

He had somehow to get her away from Luke. Every time they met Luke was there and although he liked Luke a lot he wanted to be on his own with Margaret.

Danny wondered whether to enlist Shannon's help, because it was obvious that Luke fancied Shannon but it was equally obvious to Danny that Shannon was not interested in Luke.

'I'm thinking about becoming a nun,' squashed Danny's hopes.

He could see why. Shannon was sick and tired of the bairns. When her mother had announced recently that she was pregnant again Shannon had flounced upstairs and Danny, following, found her in a bad mood.

'What is she having another baby for? Aren't there enough of us to keep?'

'We're Catholics,' Danny said.

'They should stop doing it, then,' Shannon said. 'It's the stupidest thing ever, anyroad. All my dad is good for is...' She stopped there.

Keir Logan did not beat his children but Danny thought one of these days Shannon would go too far and the rule would be broken. The ceilings were thin in their house. She did not have to shout for her dad to hear. Keir could be surprisingly deaf when he chose.

So Danny could not ask Shannon to distract Luke. He would have to get Margaret to himself somehow.

In fact it was easier than he thought. Sunday afternoon they usually got together on the beach but there was a certain Sunday in October when Jessie wasn't well so Shannon, much to her disgust, had to stay at home and see to the children. It wasn't fair but Danny wanted to be away so badly that he went without a word.

When he got there Margaret was alone, sitting at the top of the beach, well above the incoming tide. It was not in Danny's nature to rejoice that Luke had a cold so bad his mother wouldn't let him out, but he could not help being pleased at having Margaret all to himself.

They walked slowly along the beach away from the town and there was nobody about. Then they took off their shoes and paddled. The North Sea had had all summer to warm up and the day was perfect, the waves barely breaking across the soft sand.

Danny was emboldened after a short while to reach for Margaret's hand. She hesitated for a second and then gave him the hand. It was the most important event of Danny's life.

They walked and the day was still and the sun went down and as the tide came in they moved further up the beach. And when Danny couldn't bear not to any longer, when he chided himself that if he didn't do it now he might never have the opportunity again, he put his hands at either side of her waist and tried to kiss her on the mouth. She drew back immediately and stopped him.

'Don't you want me to?'

Margaret didn't answer.

'I don't know,' she said eventually.

'What do you mean? You either do or you don't.'

She looked at him.

'What if I let you and then we fall out?'

'Why would we fall out?'

Margaret raised her eyes to the heavens. 'Because that's what always happens. I've lost enough things, my dad, my house, the few friends I valued, my whole way of life. I care about you and Shannon. I don't want us to fall out because you and I... I want you and Shannon and Luke and me to be always together.'

'That isn't very realistic.' He didn't think it was preferable to the idea of kissing her either and he didn't understand how she could think so.

'I don't want to be realistic. I'm done with it.'

Danny turned his head away and watched the waves.

'Don't sulk, Danny, and don't pretend you're stupid and don't know what I mean. If we start kissing where will it stop and when it does what will we have left?'

'I don't care right now.'

'Of course you don't, you're a boy and they never think about anything else. It would be different if we were older but I've never kissed anybody in my life.'

'And you don't want to start with me? Fine,' Danny said and he got up and walked away.

She ran after him.

'You're the most important person in the world to me after Luke. Please don't fall out with me now.'

Danny stood with his head down.

'I can't help how I feel about it,' he said.

'All right but wait. Will you wait?'

'I suppose. If you like. How long?'

'I don't know. A year or so maybe. Until we leave school. Then we can do what we like and then … if you still want me–'

'I shall always want you.'

'You don't know that. You shouldn't make promises you might not be able to keep.'

'A year is a very long time,' Danny said.

And then without warning she came over and put her arms around his neck and kissed him. Danny held her close and kissed her and it was the best thing that had ever happened. Then she let go and looked into his eyes and said, 'Will you wait, then?'

'Yes, if you want me to. Can we go for a walk by ourselves sometimes?'

'I suppose.'

It was the first of several evenings. Every time she would get out somehow. He did not ask whether she told lies or slid down from her bedroom window, across the carriage-house roof and the back door into the yard and out to the field.

His mam did not notice his going until it was late and he should go to the pub for his dad. He took to calling into the Black Diamond on the way from spending the evening with Margaret.

He learned to love the beach, the sound of the waves, the way that ducks came on to the ponds just over in the dusk, and when he left her and went to the pub for his dad sometimes he and Keir would go back to the cool sands and run about there beside the rocks and celebrate being alive.

He wanted to shriek above the waves so that somehow it would go on and on and so would his feelings for Margaret. When they got older they would be able to get married and be together for always and she would belong to him completely just like his mam belonged to his dad, only better.

He was happy just to know that it would

happen. His dad was the best person to be with then because he understood about things without being told. He would run into the sea and back, he would laugh and yell Danny's name. And he knew that his dad loved him as he had loved nobody before and possibly never would again, that the love that a person had for his child was above and beyond anything that ever happened.

He kept his feelings for Margaret a secret, clutched to him in the night when Shannon and Theresa and the others slept. It was a gift, a treasure, something God-given. He wanted to be with Margaret more than he had ever wanted anything in his life.

The only job Danny could get was fishing, so because the fishermen would have him he went with them. Shannon couldn't get a job at all. Her mother said she could not do without her at home, it was too hard now that she was pregnant but when Shannon went shopping with Mary one Saturday morning she came across Miss Wilson, who she knew from Margaret was engaged to Mr Gray. Miss Wilson came over the road, smiling and said to her, 'I understand you're looking for some work. We could use some help in our house.'

Shannon didn't know what to say. Miss Wilson must know she had been dismissed from the Grays' house. Why would she want to take her on, except that all the older women were doing war work and Miss Wilson was having to run that great big vicarage on her own, her mam and dad being much older and presumably not much use?

'Mrs Gray turned me from the house,' Shannon said just in case there might be some mistake.

'Yes, I know. I thought it was a paltry reason,' Miss Wilson said, still smiling.

Paltry was a good word, Shannon thought. She was half inclined to tell Miss Wilson that her mother was pregnant again and couldn't be left but the truth was that they needed the money too much for her to stay at home when she was offered work.

'The work is hard because it's a big house but I will pay you a decent wage,' Miss Wilson said. Shannon thought it was the first time she had heard a woman talk about money like that and she liked it.

'How often would you want me there?' she said.

'How about five days, not weekends?' Phoebe said and it was settled.

Shannon bought the groceries, having

queued for so long that her feet hurt and Mary began to cry and then she trudged home to tell her mother of Miss Wilson's offer. Jessie tried to look pleased but she did not want to be left here to do everything, Shannon knew. She smiled and said, 'That's grand, Miss Wilson's nice.'

She was, Shannon thought, and then knew from her own point of view that it would be much better being at the vicarage than being at home with small children and her mother.

She started the following week and she liked it much better than she had liked being at the Grays' house. These people didn't seem to care that she was a Catholic like some people did. All they asked was how her mother did.

They sat her down at half past ten and gave her coffee and biscuits and a good dinner at one and urged her to stay when she was finished to have tea with them by the fire so that she did not have to eat at home.

And they were rich people, they had furniture it was a pleasure to polish. Mr Wilson was always coming in and smiling and telling her what a good job she was making of everything. Mrs Wilson was rather frail and lay down on her bed in the afternoons but she never complained about anything.

Miss Wilson did the work outside, she had turned the garden over to vegetables and had an allotment and very often gave Shannon food to take home, so Shannon thought it was a good thing all round and if she had not felt more guilty about it she would have wanted to go at weekends.

She liked best being out in the garden with Miss Wilson though there was a great deal of work to do in the house and they began to work together because it was more fun, she would dust and Miss Wilson would Hoover and they would prepare the vegetables having been into the garden for them and they would wash up together. It was like having an older sister, Shannon thought.

Another nice thing was that Mr Wilson had a record player and almost all day wonderful music floated through the house, piano, violin and other instruments Shannon knew nothing about, great big sounds and it made you feel better.

She did the washing on a Monday and enjoyed hanging it out and then ironing it, when it was half dry, standing in Mrs Wilson's big kitchen – until one day when Mrs Wilson came in and told her she must never stand to iron, it was so much harder work.

It had not occurred to Shannon that you could sit down to iron but that was what she did after that, because Mrs Wilson went and got the big white stool out of the back kitchen and brought it in for her.

As it was she ended up cleaning at home and doing the washing on Saturdays, because you couldn't wash on Sundays, it just wasn't right.

People would be scandalized if you hung out washing and Shannon cared very much for it being a holy day. She went to church twice, partly just to get away in the evening, but she loved the ceremony of the mass, the peacefulness of being there and the idea that one day she might be able to devote her whole life to this.

Luke and Margaret were aware that the Logans needed help and spent what money they had on any extras which they could get, considering rationing, for Sunday afternoons when they took the children to the beach.

'May I have an advance on my pocket money?' Luke asked Callum.

'It comes through the bank, I can't advance you it.'

'Then can you give me some anyway?'

'Why?'

'I spent all of it.'

'On what?'

Luke shrugged. Callum, to his surprise, gave him the money. He went to his uncle the week after and asked again for money. He was even more surprised to be given it.

He and Margaret trudged to the Logan house only to find, when they got there, that Callum had followed them.

'Is this where my money's going?' he said, as he walked in by the back door, past the pantry and stepped down into the kitchen. 'Why are you...?' and then he stopped.

Jessie Logan paused halfway down the stairs. It seemed to Luke that she stood there for a long time but it could have been just seconds. She glanced around at the children and then her gaze came to rest on Luke's uncle.

'Mr Gray,' she said, her voice flat. 'Would you like a cup of tea?'

It was just a split second before Callum answered equably, 'That would be nice.'

She looked, what was the word? Luke thought, as she came downstairs. Yes, he had remembered it. Regal. She looked queenly, like she had robes and not like a poor woman with too many children.

It was Margaret's idea that they should go to the beach and take the children. Danny was like a thunder cloud but he didn't say anything.

Cal was glad of the respite.

The minute the outside door closed on the children Jessie said, 'What in the hell do you want?' just as though they were all sixteen again and it had been only days and not years since they had met.

'Can I come in?'

'If you must.' She shifted the baby on to the other hip.

Inside she had obviously made an effort but poverty had bettered her. There was not a decent stick of furniture in the place. The baby began to cry. She paced up and down for a while and then the baby slept. She put it into a pram at the far side of the room in the shadows and came back to him.

'Do you know that Danny's seeing Margaret?'

'Like I've got nowt else to do, Callum.' He didn't know what to say. 'Who's Margaret?'

'Margaret is Ailsa and Jaime's daughter, the girl who just went off to the beach with him.'

'She's what?' Jessie held his gaze scornfully.

'You must know. He died–'

'I knew that.'

'Ailsa brought the children back here–'

'And you let her?'

'It is their home.'

'And our Danny's seeing this lass?'

'Yes.'

'Has he been with her?'

'I don't know.'

'Aye,' she said heavily, 'I remember you at sixteen, you and your brother. You've developed a short memory since you became so important. Don't you remember going with me, then, Callum?'

'Yes,' he said softly.

'What?'

'I said yes! But it was him, wasn't it?'

Her gaze faltered for the first time.

'I don't know what you mean,' she said.

'Danny is Jaime's child.'

'He's Keir's bairn.'

'He is not.'

'You're the only one that thinks it, then. And whatever gave you such a daft notion?'

'He loved you and Danny is the spit of him. For God's sake. He looks more like me than he does like Keir.'

'You aren't much on biology, are you?' she said. 'It's got nothing to do with love.'

'So you won't do anything about it.'

'Like what?' She held his gaze so fiercely that he wanted to run.

'Do you want me to tell Ailsa?'

'That's your problem.'

'And if things get more involved and there's a child?'

'I don't know how you find time to worry about so many things. You think I'm going to turn round to our Danny and tell him what to do?

'Do you know something, Cal? There's an awful lot of folks who are related close and sleep together. Maybe in your world that's so polite, though God knows how you survive in it, people do the right thing but I think you're kidding yourself.

'You can put coats and coats of whitewash on things but they only look different because of it and I'll tell you summat else that I don't think you know.

'You were my first. Your brother was a long time after. I thought I cared about you but to you I was just some nasty cheap little lass who had nowt and was there to be had for the taking–'

'That's not right.'

'Isn't it? I hadn't even a pair of shoes.'

'You wanted me to offer you money?'

'I wanted you to offer me some respect. You went with me and then you ignored me.'

'They sent me away to school to get me out of the way.'

'All right, I'll let you off, then, considering, but don't come up here in your posh suit and think you're better than everybody else—'

'I don't.'

The baby began to cry again. She went over and picked it out of the pram.

'You hadn't even the decency to marry. You know what your trouble was? You had to have everything your brother had. Just as well you had me first, isn't it? Did you tell him?'

'Of course I didn't.'

'Not even when he took the lass you finally wanted? You didn't know I knew? Hm? Everybody knew. You didn't marry because of her. Well, you can have her now, now he's finished with her. I don't suppose for a minute she was enough for him. Nowt was ever enough for him.'

'You seemed to like him well enough.'

Jessie held her head high.

'I never loved nobody but Keir. Your

123

brother was just a … he was nowt and as for you…'

She didn't finish the sentence. Callum held her eyes unflinchingly. She laughed.

'You were nice,' she said, relenting. 'I cried for a week. Did your dad send you away on purpose?'

'Maybe. I don't know now. I hated that school. You really loved Keir?'

'Oh God, yes.'

'You were lucky.'

'Aye, I suppose I was.'

'You haven't changed at all, you're still so beautiful.'

She laughed again.

'Stop being so nice to me.'

'Tell Danny if he comes to the foundry I'll give him a job.'

She looked amazed. 'You would?'

'Talk to him.'

'I'm saying nowt to Danny. Let them alone, why don't you? They'll have little enough time for such things.'

Callum held her eyes with his gaze. There was suddenly silence and she was looking beyond him and the look told him exactly that Keir Logan was standing in the doorway.

Callum cursed himself. He hadn't heard. For a drunk and a foundryman Keir was abnormally quiet in his movements when he chose. Cal took a deep breath and turned around, inwardly yelling at himself for not thinking that her husband might choose to come home. Presumably the midday session was over at the pub, it was mid-afternoon after all, so Keir would be back to sleep it off before the evening.

Keir looked levelly at him and Cal was amazed, not for the first time, that Keir could be so genial sometimes and then like this, when all but the very brave would get out of his presence as fast as possible. Cal attempted a smile, remembered he was this man's employer and said in what he hoped was a friendly voice, 'Hello, Keir.'

'Mr Gray.' And then Keir looked at Jessie.

There was just a hint that Keir knew he had stumbled on to a private conversation and since it was rare in those parts for a woman to have secrets from her husband Cal was going to have to be very careful.

'I came to talk about Danny.'

'When I wasn't here?'

Cal knew he was going to have to try and take charge of this conversation or there was going to be some kind of fight. Logan was famous for his fighting, both verbal and physical, the Irish in him making him handy with his tongue, so it was a foolhardy man who took him on. If he started fighting with his employer he would lose his job and after that they would lose everything.

'You're hardly ever at home,' Cal said firmly, 'I wasn't going to wait around for you to show your face.'

The seconds passed. Keir moved into the kitchen. It hadn't been a big room before he got there but with the three of them, all seemingly hostile, it had shrunk to the size of a coalhouse.

'I thought I might offer Danny a job.'

'What do you know about it?' It wasn't quite threatening because in Keir's deceptively soft Irish tone it was just a question.

'I know he was at the pit and isn't any more.'

'He's fishing. He likes it,' Jessie said and Cal was so grateful for her intervention that he smiled at her.

'It can't pay much, though, does it? I'm sure I can do better.'

'A recent acquaintance, is it?' Keir said.

'He comes to the house, he and Luke play football.' He didn't say that they were drinking his whisky and smoking his Capstans. He decided that the best attack here was defence.

'If you don't think it's a good idea it doesn't matter, but if you want to talk to Danny about it you could send him to see me,' Cal said and he left.

It wasn't until he got outside that he let go of his breath.

The baby had gone to sleep. Jessie went on with what she had been doing before her visitor arrived, making the tea.

'Isn't it ready?' Keir said, as though he was always on time for meals.

She looked sideways at him.

'You should've come back for your dinner,' she said reprovingly.

He caught hold of her from behind and kissed her neck.

'I got talking to Joe Hobson. Make us me tea, Jessie.'

'Do you want a thick ear?' she said and it was exactly the right thing to say. He laughed and all the tension went from the room.

He washed and changed and Shannon and Danny came back in and Jessie hoped that Keir had forgotten about it. When they had eaten, Keir pushed his chair sideways from the table and said to Danny, 'Mr Gray came by. He wants to offer you a job at the foundry.'

127

'Who, me?' Danny stared, surprised.

'No, our Shannon. Don't be soft.'

'Does he really?'

'You sound pleased.'

'Well, I am. Can I?'

'If you like.'

'When?'

'He didn't say. You could come in the morning and I could take you to the office.'

'That'd be grand,' Danny said.

Jessie was almost asleep when Keir, whom she had thought asleep, said without moving, 'So, what did Cal Gray really want?'

Jessie didn't reply. She had her back to him. Keir turned her over.

'Well?'

'I don't know what you mean.'

'Yes, you do.'

'He wanted me to leave you and go and be his fancy piece. He doesn't mind that I have five kids and a wrecked body because of it, or that I'm pregnant.'

Keir didn't say anything to that, which she thought was good.

'Would you rather our Danny went fishing than to the works?'

'No.'

'Well, then.' He didn't speak, and she

thought for a man who was good with words Keir was much better with his silences. It was enough to break anybody unwary in two but she had lived with him for a long time. She said, 'I love you. I've never loved anybody but you and that's saying a lot considering how you go on. Somewhere in you, Keir Logan, there's a decent man but he's swimming in beer.'

'I didn't go to the pub tonight,' he said, as though she didn't know, but then she had been surprised and had said nothing.

'Why, were you too frightened Cal Gray was going to come back while you weren't here?'

'He wouldn't dare,' Keir said and then he kissed her.

Jessie loved his kisses more than anything on earth. He knew how to get it exactly right. His lovemaking was wonderful. It was a shame he couldn't apply the same standards to the rest of his life, she thought. But he had doubted her.

The following night Keir went to the pub. It was the Black Diamond, his favourite. He would have spent his whole life there if he could have, getting sweetly drunk so that the world looked good, or at least the world around him, the one small smoky room with its coal fire, its brown walls, brown floor, brown bar, brown ale.

Velvet, nectar, easing the world along, pushing away any nasty thoughts. He played darts or dominoes or just sat looking into the fire, thinking what a wonderful world it was. The company was good and beyond it he could hear the beach, the waves, the wind and all those things which had belonged to his childhood, when his mother was alive and he had lain in bed in the back room and watched the stars from the window.

It was gone but he had the quiet of the Saturday and Sunday afternoons, when there was one o'clock and two o'clock and best of all somehow, three o'clock, the very antithesis of three o'clock in the morning.

The few times he had been near enough to hear some sodding clock striking it out for all to hear, he had thought, it was indecent.

The time when you imagined you would die. The time you thought of all the people you loved who had died. The time when the night was broken in two halves and it was dark – even in June here in the north where the light was at its best, soft beyond the windows, beyond the curtains, if there were any – it was dark then and it brought with it all the horrors of your life, every last guilt-ridden thing you had done was presented mercilessly before your eyes.

Even through the haze of beer and coal fires he could see that it was his own fault. It was his own stupidity which had brought him to the fire and the beer and the afternoons and the evenings and he had grown used to it, liked it, could no longer imagine that things could be better.

When it was late he sang his way home. He sang 'Danny Boy', it seemed appropriate. He liked Danny. He liked everybody. The road home was as soft as a feather pillow. Nobody was up when he got there. All he had to do was crawl into bed and fall into the kind of blessed sleep which did not allow three o'clock. He felt smug about that.

Ten

Ailsa went to the office. It was the first time she had been there and it reminded her how Jaime had always hated the place. She had not thought the works could be so big and confusing. She could see sheds in front of her, various buildings with doors open, and had to ask her way.

They seemed to know who she was. The man in the main office directed her, opened the door, sent her down a small passage where the sun came in through dusty windows until she reached his door.

Cal was sitting behind the desk and got up when he saw her. It was, she decided, a very businesslike office. He looked surprised to see her and also he looked different. Were men different at work?

Perhaps Jaime had been. He must have been because he was successful but then he had been charming and intelligent, that was enough to get some people through.

His eyes held a hint of impatience, as though he was busy, and when he got up

133

from the desk, as he did simply for manners' sake, he was Jaime for a few seconds. It was somehow, in the intricacy of family likenesses, a graceful shadow and reminded her of things she would rather have forgotten.

During those few moments she couldn't remember what she was doing and she could see also the huge difference between the two men. Jaime had loved elegant clothes, had cared for order in the home, warmth, comfort, good food, linen tablecloths, formality. In fact, she thought, he had been a sensualist, which was why he had attracted women so easily.

Cal was the very opposite. The house he now owned was vast and echoing with high ceilings and long halls, old-fashioned furniture and shabby curtains, and the food was basic. There were no special comforts, no treats. Perhaps if it were not wartime it would be different, but somehow she didn't think so.

The only concession, and she was grateful for it, because the bedrooms were big enough to be bitter in cold weather, was that because they lived in a coal field there was a fire in every downstairs room and because the place was so big they had privacy, a bedroom each, enough space to get away from one another.

It had a drawing room, a sitting room, a sewing room, a tiny room lined with bookshelves where Margaret spent much of her time, a music room where they often sat in the evenings and a billiard room where Luke did, and a study, where Cal retreated in the evenings. There was the dining room where they ate and the kitchen was enormous, tiled in blue and white with various small rooms off it with sinks and shelving and storage and outside there were lots of outbuildings and gardens and fields which belonged to the house for when there had been carriages and horses. It could not be said to be luxurious in any sense.

She thought Cal was shrewd, clever and there was plenty of money. Men like him made money out of war, not deliberately, she did not think he was like that, but just because of the work they did.

His office was dusty and crowded with filing cabinets, ledgers on shelves at the back, piles of papers on his desk, an in-tray overflowing, a spike which wouldn't take any more, as though he never reached the end of what he was doing and since he had been overworked for almost four years the light, if there had ever been any – she couldn't remember – had gone from his eyes.

She thought it was understandable that he should look warily at her before he asked her to sit down and he was right of course. She would hardly come to his office like this bearing good news.

Her seat was opposite to him across the narrow desk and he offered her tea, which she declined. The sun made the window look even dirtier. The view was of foundry buildings, she had no idea what they were, and from there also men went by from time to time, heads down, intent on work, up and across the dusty path between the buildings.

He didn't say anything more after the offer of tea, he just sat there and waited for her to convey the bad news, like somebody who knew there was no point in hurrying her towards it, was happy of even a few moments' grace before the axe fell. Cal, she thought, had had none of the pleasures of life, he had merely inherited other people's errors.

'Margaret is... I suppose you think I should have waited until you came home...'

'Not at all,' Cal said and she wondered whether the polite veneer was ever going to fall away.

'It's just that at home one can never be sure of not being overheard and it's vital that…' She glanced at the door.

Cal waited.

'Margaret is … is spending a great deal of time with Keir Logan's boy.' Why call him that now, she thought? How stupid.

'Yes, I know. They do seem to get through an amazing quantity of whisky and cigarettes.'

Ailsa stared at him. That Cal should know more about her children than she did was somehow not right.

'They're smoking and drinking?'

'They could be doing worse. In fact they probably are,' Cal said, with a hint of resignation.

'They're fifteen next month.'

'Didn't you smoke and drink at that age?'

'Certainly not,' Ailsa said.

'No, I expect you were busy playing Mozart and being nice to your mother.'

'I was,' Ailsa said, recollecting the last years of her mother's illness. 'And Luke?'

'Oh, especially Luke.'

'He's just like Jaime was,' Ailsa said with a sigh.

Cal didn't say, 'Let's hope not,' but somehow the words breached the silence between them.

'I don't want Margaret to see Danny,'

Ailsa said.

'No?' Cal considered. 'And how do you propose to stop it?'

'What do you mean?'

'Well … I have the feeling that opposition will only make the problem worse. Danny is a nice lad. Jessie has done well with her two eldest children. Shannon is such a modest bright girl and Danny will make a very good foundryman, I think. I'm hoping he'll agree to go to night classes–'

'They're Catholics,' Ailsa said, desperately hoping this might be enough to explain her remarks.

'Is saying that to Margaret going to help?'

'Keir Logan drinks.'

'Or that?'

Ailsa stopped there and waited but he just sat and looked at her. She said, 'Cal…' then lapsed into the silence. When neither her protestations nor the mention of his name had helped or brought from him any response she said, 'Danny Logan is Jaime's son.'

Through the window she could hear the noise of the nearest big buildings, clanking and running like engines and a man shouting to another some indecipherable instruction or remark.

'What makes you think so?' Cal said softly.

'After he died I found some old papers, an old diary. He was in love with her. I don't think he ever loved me.' It hurt to say all this but somehow it hurt less as she went on.

It was something she had known for years but not spoken of. Cal was like some wretched priest in a confessional, she ended up telling him everything. 'I think that was why he went with other women.'

Ailsa, afraid she might begin to cry, almost got up and then didn't. 'I was too serious, had spent too much time around sickrooms. He told me once that I smelled of it, all that … pain, all those endless afternoons.'

'Jessie loved Keir.'

'Yes, I'm sure. But we make mistakes.'

'I think you should leave well alone.'

'But what if he … what if they … I don't think we can afford to take chances.'

She stopped there, realizing something.

'You knew. You knew all along.' She waited for him to deny it. 'Oh God. He asked me to marry him because Jessie wouldn't and she was pregnant. He was sleeping with her when he … and you…' Ailsa tried to get out of the office.

Cal stopped her, put his hands on her arms. It was the first time he had touched her in almost twenty years.

'You can't run out of here like this. There are people in the front office. Stay there.'

Once she had agreed and sat down he opened the door and Ailsa, trembling, heard him ask for some tea. He came back and talked to her, soft indecipherable words, none of which she remembered afterwards. When the tea came she sat staring into her cup as though it were poisoned.

'I can't believe you asked me to marry you out of pity.'

'It wasn't out of pity,' Cal said.

'Oh, no. It was to stop me from marrying Jaime, so that Jessie would come to her senses and have him.'

'It wasn't for that.'

'What was it for, then?'

He hesitated and then he said, 'Jessie was never going to marry anybody but Keir.'

And then she thought she understood fully. He had loved Jaime and had not wanted him to make mistakes.

'It was a long time ago,' he said.

Ailsa sighed and drank her tea and when it was done she put down the cup and saucer on the desk and said, 'I don't want Margaret mixed up in anything which might hurt her. Jessie Logan will have to be told. Will you

140

speak to her?'

He looked away at the window for a few seconds.

'You think I should wait until Margaret is expecting a baby and then sort the bigger mess?' Ailsa said. 'If he's anything like his father, Danny will seduce her.'

Still Cal said nothing.

'If you aren't going to do something about this—'

'I've already done it,' he said, meeting her eyes. Ailsa stared.

'You talked to Jessie about it?'

'Yes, I did.'

'Without telling me.'

'I didn't know whether you knew.'

'What did she say?'

'She will talk to Danny.'

'Then I must speak to Margaret,' Ailsa said and she left.

'You ought not to see Danny Logan,' Margaret's mother said.

Margaret looked at her. Firstly she hadn't realized her mother knew she was spending time with Danny and secondly she hadn't thought her mother would mind. One of her few good traits, Margaret had always thought, was that she was not a snob. She had never tried to choose their friends.

'I'm sure Danny's very nice,' her mother was saying, 'but...'

'But what? Is it because he works for us? Mr Blandford, the manager, has told him he'll do very well.'

'I'm sure,' her mother said.

There was another 'but' coming up, Margaret felt certain, and even though her mother didn't say it she heard it.

Was it because Danny was a Catholic whereas they trudged down Church Lane to the parish church every Sunday morning? Margaret knew that she did a great many things her mother would disapprove of but usually her mother didn't know so there was no dispute. Margaret was not used to dealing with opposition from her. Also, to give her mother credit, she didn't usually make a fuss about nothing, so what was her point?

'Why shouldn't I see him?'

'Do you know his family?'

'I know Shannon well enough.'

'Danny's father drinks.' She didn't mean he had a couple of whiskies in the evening while he worked in the study like Cal did. Ailsa was too polite to say 'Keir Logan is a drunk'.

'That's not Danny's fault,' she said.

142

'No, no, I'm not saying it is, but Danny must feel the responsibility for his family. There are a lot of them and they don't have much money.'

'I don't understand what your point is,' Margaret said, even though she did. She nearly talked of Danny as a friend and then didn't. Her mother was not stupid. She knew what was going on. Margaret felt as though she could not exist another day without Danny. She was surprised at herself. How quickly she had come to depend on Danny's presence in her life.

'I know that you like him but there are good reasons why you ought not to become too attached to him.'

'Attached to him? It makes me sound like a button on a coat. I don't know what you mean. Why don't you explain it to me?'

'I cannot. You'll have to trust me.'

'I can't think of a single good reason why I shouldn't see him. Did Uncle Cal say so because Danny is a foundry worker?'

'No.'

'But this is Cal's doing?'

Her mother frowned but she knew that was only because without the prefix he sounded human. Which he hardly was, Margaret thought, angry now that she had discovered the cause of the problem.

'I don't understand how people can be so unalike. Daddy was so lovely and Uncle Cal is…' She couldn't call Cal a bastard in front of her mother but he was, so very obviously. She knew without doubt that this was all Cal's fault. He had spoken to her mother about it and since her mother always listened to him they had come to this.

'He knows nothing about it, he isn't used to young people,' her mother said and Margaret heard the break in her voice and she sounded just like the times she had defended Jaime.

Her mother surely couldn't feel about her uncle as she had felt about her father. He was nothing like. Her father had been funny, kind, warm, generous, had played games with them when they were little, bought them fantastic presents.

It was only since the war came that he had changed and was rarely at home. Cal was always working even when he came back to the house. He was quiet, withdrawn even. Margaret was glad of it mostly. He barely seemed to notice what they were doing any more. Why must he interfere now and why on earth should their mother want anything to do with him?

'You must promise me,' her mother said, 'that you won't see Danny again.'

And she promised just to get away.

Danny was late in and at first he thought his mam had waited up for him because she was cross with him but as he got into the kitchen he could see that she had been crying. He wished in a way that he had not come home. Every time he came back there seemed to be a new problem and he seemed to have to sort it out.

'Where's our Shannon?' he said, hoping Shannon was still about and would be there to help.

'In bed.'

'And my dad?'

'He hasn't come back yet.' That made Danny feel guilty. He knew very well that if he didn't go to collect his dad his dad would stay out and get even more drunk than usual. 'I want to talk to you, Danny.'

His heart sank. There really must be something the matter.

'I want you not to see Margaret Gray any more,' his mam said.

Danny looked at her. He was surprised and not very pleased that she had found out he and Margaret were spending time together. How on earth did she know?

'What for?'

'Because.'

'Because what?'

'Because you're far too young to get involved with a lass. I want you to promise me you won't see her.'

'I don't see why I should.'

'You have to,' she said.

It was the way she said it that worried him.

'What for?' he said again.

'I can't tell you.'

'If you don't then I cannot stop.'

She spent what seemed to him like a long time deliberating.

'If I tell you, you must swear that you won't tell nobody because it's a secret and if it gets out … it will ruin us all.'

Danny wished he could have stayed out all night. Things had been so much less complicated when he was with Margaret. He wanted to run back to the beach and for her still to be there.

'I couldn't tell you this if I didn't think you would go ahead and lie with that lass.'

Danny didn't know where to look. What did his mam want to say such things for?

'You haven't already, have you?' she said.

Danny wanted to blurt out that no of

146

course he hadn't, but he didn't. Annoyed now he said, 'Just say what you have to say.'

She didn't look at him.

'Your dad and me courted for years and at one point we had a fight and he went off with somebody else. He took this other girl to a dance and I … I… Jaime Gray fancied me and I…'

Danny didn't have to hear any more. His mother had gone with Mr Gray, Margaret's dad. How disgusting.

'I don't want to know,' he said, making for the stairs.

She got hold of his sleeve. She was crying openly now and he was half-inclined to run.

'I had you because of it,' she said.

Margaret waited and waited for Danny on the beach the following day. There really must be something the matter and Danny must know all about it too because he would need a really good reason not to show up, she thought, more worried than ever.

The following day, at half past five, when the men trudged out of the foundry gates she stood, waiting. He must have seen her but he didn't acknowledge her, though a lot of the men eyed her with surprise or curiosity.

Not caring, she ran after him, past the Salvation Army citadel and up the steep hill beyond the bank. Finally she got hold of his arm so that Danny was obliged to stop or deliberately push her from him.

She had the awful feeling he would pretend there was nothing wrong or say that he didn't want to see her any more or try to brush her off in some way. But he didn't, he just stood there with his grubby brown face from his hard day, his dusty clothes, his thick black hair streaked with dirt, he stood and looked across the road at the fields which led to the sea.

'I know there's something wrong,' she said. 'Why didn't you come and tell me?'

Danny stood like a statue and didn't say anything and didn't look at her. Margaret had seen that look before and it frightened her. Then he said in a tired voice, 'I just don't want to see you any more, all right?'

'No, it isn't all right,' Margaret said, angry rather than crying. 'If you don't want to see somebody any more you tell them, you don't just … just... And anyhow, I don't believe it.'

'It's true,' Danny said, his voice hard and flat. 'I've got a lass, somebody a lot prettier than you. She's got yellow hair and blue eyes and she's nice to me.'

'Nice to you?'

Danny finally looked at her.

'She lets me do things to her,' he said.

Margaret had no idea she was going to hit him round the ear for that but she did and she said, not caring if anybody heard, 'You bloody liar, Danny Logan, you've got nothing of the sort.'

'I have!' Danny shot back at her but his eyes were no longer steady and when she glared at him he turned away.

Margaret glared back at him so hard that it made him look at her.

'I want to know the real reason and then if you like I won't see you.'

His eyes lost all the distance in them and she saw the warmth that was present only for her. He still didn't say anything but it didn't matter now because she could see her reflection deep within his dark eyes.

'Meet me at the beach later,' she said and then she turned and walked off, confident in the knowledge that he would be there.

Danny walked. He didn't go home, he couldn't. He didn't want to see his mother, the look in her eyes, and he certainly didn't want her to see the expression in his face, reckless, careless.

He went to the beach and waited there as the tide crashed up the sand, until Margaret met him, and then he drew her in amongst the dunes and told her what his mother had told him. All the time she sat there, her hands clutching his hands and her face gradually paling until it was whiter than the breaking waves' foam up the shore. And after he had told her she got to her feet and she said, 'It isn't true. My dad would never have done such a thing, never.'

'My mam wouldn't lie to me, especially about something which could make such a mess of everything,' Danny said.

'She's got it wrong, Danny. Look at you, you look exactly like your dad. Somebody's doing this on purpose, probably my Uncle Callum because he's a complete bugger. I'm going to find him and I'm going to tell him what I think of him–'

'Margaret–'

He tried to get hold of her but she ran, and the more he called after her the faster she scurried up the beach and out of sight.

Margaret ran all the way back to the village but not home. She ran down the street and through the puddles where the surfaced road gave way to unmade road just outside the foundry and down past the back lane and across the path where the foundry buildings began.

She burst into the office. It was deserted. She didn't stop there, she ran down the narrow passage and hauled open the door of Cal's office. He was there, of course, he was always there unless he was at home. As he looked up she shouted at him.

'My dad didn't do it, he couldn't have. He would never have done such things and you are a bugger for saying it!' She paused there, taking a breath, waiting for Cal to say something. When he didn't she went on, 'You're just jealous because he was better than you and he had a wife and children and he was kind and funny and generous and all the things that you aren't. You shouldn't be saying such things.

'You just don't want me to go around with Danny because he's Irish and – and because they don't have any money and because...' She couldn't go on, the tears threatened.

There was silence in the office. She couldn't even hear the men outside because they had long since gone home. It was mid-evening. She couldn't bear the silence. She needed Cal to tell her that it was true, that her dad had adored her mother and his children and would never in a thousand years have done such a thing, but he didn't.

She wished she could leave. She wished she could run away from him as she had run away from Danny but she was beginning to understand now that however much you ran the truth would follow you and it was the truth.

She wanted to go on shouting at Cal, at anybody, that Jaime would not have done such a thing, that he loved his family better than anything in the world, but in the moments when Cal sat there looking at her and not saying anything she admitted to herself for the first time that it was not true.

Their dad might have liked them when they were little but he hadn't for a very long time, he had avoided them, hadn't wanted to spend time with them however much they tried to get him to and it was the hardest thing on earth when you loved somebody and they didn't love you.

She felt as though she hated everybody, her dad for doing such an awful thing, Cal for knowing and not telling them, Danny for being who he now was, Danny's mam for being a loose bitch and her own mother for not having the guts to tell her what was wrong. Everything came together in her mind like a big wall that was crashing over with a huge force behind it.

Her dad was dead and he had made a mess of things, just like, she acknowledged, he had always made a mess of things. She and Luke had gone on and on loving him like they were throwing their affection for him into a big empty space. They hardly ever saw him and he had made her mother so very unhappy. Why had he not loved them?

Even though he was so unreliable, so mean with his time and his affection, they had gone on caring, gone on hoping even for a few minutes with him, like hungry people waiting for crumbs, and it had never happened.

Her dad had never liked her, not really, she was not feminine enough, not pretty enough, her dad wanted her to be dainty and able to wear stupid pastel shades and she couldn't. The idea of how she had been an unnatural little girl got the better of her and she burst into tears. Her dad was dead and she would never be the child he had wanted.

For a few moments she stood there, lost, alone, unloved, unwanted with nowhere to go. Then Cal got up as though to come to her and once he was on his feet the action freed her. She threw herself at him.

She had never done such a thing in her life. There had been many times when she had wanted her dad to hold her, to protect her, but she had known with a sure child's instinct that Jaime was not the man to protect anybody, so she had held back all those years while he went around making a mess of things and spoiling their lives.

He had ruined her childhood and her mother's life with his stupid carelessness and now he had spoiled the most important thing of all and she couldn't bear it. She couldn't go back to the house like this, her mother had had enough but Cal could stand it, she knew he could.

She was, for a second or two after she had done it, horribly embarrassed but unable to move away, and then he put his arms around her and after that she kept her face in against the dusty shoulder of his jacket which smelled of the foundry, the odd smell of the sharp sand which they used for the castings, quite different from ordinary beach sand. She would never think of it the same again and all around them she felt that the world had come to an end.

She clung but Cal was safe, she knew he

was, and it was a very strange feeling, safe enough to be accused when the tears had stopped and she ventured away from his shoulder.

'Why didn't you tell me?' she said looking up into his concerned eyes.

'It wasn't my place to tell you,' Cal said, moving back slightly. 'Did your mother?'

'No, Danny. His mother said. How could my dad do such a thing?'

'Everybody makes mistakes. Some just have bigger repercussions than others.'

'Why are you so nice about him? He never liked you. Are you going to pretend that you liked him?'

'He's dead,' Cal said.

Margaret sniffed, fingered the lapel of his jacket.

'What am I going to do?'

'You just go on from day to day like everybody else does.'

'Are you going to get rid of Danny?'

'Do you want me to?'

'It isn't his fault. He didn't do anything. I wouldn't like him to be put out of his job, that would just make things worse.' She looked into his eyes and thought for the first time that they were very nice eyes, rather cool but sympathetic at present.

'I don't want to. I think he's going to be very good in time.'

'Are you coming back for tea? It's late.'

'I think I'd better.'

Margaret drew away.

'I'm sorry I did that, I know I'm too big and you maybe think that I–'

'I don't think anything of the sort. It's all right,' he said.

'Are you sure?'

'Quite sure.'

They left the works and walked slowly back to the house and it was nice walking with him because he didn't say anything. When they reached the hall Margaret ran away from him up the stairs and into her bedroom, she was so ashamed of herself.

Eleven

If Jessie could have thought of a way to tell Keir that Danny was not his son she would have done so. Too many people knew the truth for it to remain a secret and she dreaded what he would do when he found out, but there was no way you could tell a man you had been married to for more than fifteen years that his only son was another man's child.

She was about seven months pregnant, the baby was big for her and maybe that would prevent Keir from killing her, she didn't know. What she had always loved best about him was that you never knew with him, except that he had not been violent with her or the children.

He did his fighting in the streets at night and but for the bruises, the broken skin across his knuckles and the odd smear of blood, he seemed to manage quite well, just as he did with the drink, it was a part of his life, it always had been. They didn't talk about it.

This was the biggest problem she had ever faced and she had no idea what to do about it. In the end she went to the foundry office and was ushered into Cal Gray's office. He looked levelly at her stomach from where he sat at the far side of the desk and then he got up and offered her a chair.

'I think I know what this is about,' he said.

'Aye, I dare say. He's going to kill me when he finds out,' Jessie said, sitting down.

'I'm glad you told Danny.'

She looked severely at him. 'Will you be glad when Keir wrings my neck? He will, you know.'

'Do you want me to tell him?'

'Oh, that'll be a big help,' she said, 'he'll kill you first and then me.'

'There's got to be a way round it.'

'I would love to hear it. Danny knows, Margaret, and presumably Ailsa, you and me. How long before it gets out and the whole world knows? What do I say – "I'm terribly sorry but I married you when I was having another lad's bairn and you've kept it, thinking it was yours, your only son"?

'He'll murder me. And Danny. Keir had an awful life before he met me and look what I've done to him. I feel like running away and taking the bairns with me.'

158

'Not very practical.'

'And how practical do you think it will be for my children when their mother is dead and their father is hanged for killing her? Who's going to take them in, you? They'll end up in some orphanage.' She glanced at Cal but he wasn't looking at her. 'Danny's heartbroken,' she said. 'He loves his dad. He loves being the only lad and that Keir is so proud of him. Damn Jaime. He was always useless.'

'Maybe we should wait. He doesn't know. I don't think we're going to gain anything by telling him and if everybody is sworn to secrecy then maybe it won't get out.'

'Oh, aye?'

'What else is there to do?'

'I don't know. I thought you might have some ideas.'

'Let's just sit on the secret for now.'

'All right.' She sighed.

'Tired?'

'This is my sixth.'

'I can give you a cup of tea.'

'I have to get back. I left the bairns to our Shannon's tender mercies. She's decided she'd rather be a nun than like this. I can't imagine why. Maybe I should have thought of it,' and she smiled bleakly at him and went home.

'Is our Danny all right?'

Jessie looked up from where she was washing the plates in the sink. Shannon stood in the doorway which led into the other room.

'As far as I know,' Jessie said.

'He didn't come home last night.'

'He was here this morning and went to work, that's all I care about.'

She was glad of the job she had to do so that she wouldn't have to look at Shannon and lie. It was bad enough doing it anyroad. And then she thought, I confessed the sin at the time, that I had slept with Jaime and then about the baby.

I told Father Keeley and was forgiven. Since then I've tried not to think about it. What is it they say? Be sure your sins will find you out. Even after you've repented and been forgiven? Her sin was certainly coming back to haunt her.

Danny had not quite been lying about the blonde girl. She was the lass behind the bar in the pub. Not the pub his dad was so keen on, he wouldn't have dared go there. He went to another pub, neatly placed further along the harbour, and it was called the

Fisherman's Arms.

It had a reputation for being rough and as far as he knew none of his dad's friends, nobody who knew him, went there. His dad. Would he ever stop thinking of Keir as his dad? But of course he was in a lot of ways. Keir had always been his dad, had brought him up. He wanted more desperately than ever to be Keir's son.

It was funny, really. He was the son of a man who came from the richest family in the area whereas what he wanted to be was the son of a drunk. He loved Keir, adored him, had always respected him in spite of his faults. Keir had never hidden his faults but one of his greatest qualities was how much he loved his family and Danny knew he was the favourite. It was difficult not to be glad of that.

Not that Keir had ever said so and the girls loved their dad as well. Danny didn't know what Jaime Gray had been like as a father but from what he had gathered he hadn't been much of one.

He hadn't been much of a man either, Danny thought. He had been a bastard and not like Luke and Margaret called their Uncle Cal. Cal Gray was a sort of admirable bastard, good in business, good with money, good with people.

He had certainly been good with Danny but perhaps he had a definite purpose in mind, perhaps he had been good to Danny because Danny was Jaime's son. Danny didn't think so, he would give Mr Gray the benefit of the doubt but he thought it might have influenced him in some ways.

Danny just couldn't stay at home. He couldn't meet his dad's eyes any more. He couldn't go to the pub and collect him and be happy walking back with the sound of waves crashing across the front and know that he was in the right place. He wasn't.

He should have been up at the big house with Margaret and Luke, only not as he had wanted and still wanted to be with Margaret. So he went to the pub and walked tall – he didn't need to worry, he was nearly six foot by now and looked older than his years – and they served him beer and he thought he was Keir's son in one way, he certainly liked beer.

The pretty lass behind the bar told him he could walk her home if he wanted to and so he stayed until the end of the evening, until late when she had washed up the glasses and tidied round and the landlord told her she could go.

Then they walked down the empty pavements together in the darkness and when he got up the winding hill away from the village nearly to where she lived, Danny got hold of her in the darkness and kissed her and pretended she was Margaret.

She was nothing like Margaret. Margaret would never have let him put his hands on her legs like that. Margaret would never let him have her up against a wall. Margaret, Danny thought later, as he threw up on the front, would have been disgusted with him.

He slept on the beach. He couldn't go home, he was too guilty, too drunk, too hurt.

Margaret wanted to tell Luke. Up to now she had told him everything, except the details of her meetings with Danny. She was aware that Luke knew she was meeting Danny without him and that he felt left out, but he cared too much about her to say anything. She was glad of that but she missed Danny so much the ache was physical.

She managed to get through two days before Luke asked tentatively, 'Have you and Danny fallen out?'

'Something like that, yes. I think he's got a girl.'

'Has he?' Luke frowned. He was insulted

for her but in a way she wished that Luke would go to Danny, so that at least Danny wouldn't lose both of them. She wished she had thought of something else to say because this put Danny in the wrong when he hadn't done anything.

'I didn't think it was like that with you and Danny,' Luke said.

'It wasn't.'

'So what does it matter if he has a girl?'

Luke, she thought, silently cursing, knew her too well. He was staring. She deliberately didn't meet his gaze. Secrets were awful things. She hadn't thought before now. To have a secret from Luke was unprecedented.

Also it had not occurred to her that Luke was jealous of the time she spent with Danny. They were close. In a way Danny had breached that closeness but in another way the closeness had been breached more by the secret.

She was half afraid that Luke would go on realizing something was very badly wrong but in boy fashion, she decided, he didn't, or didn't choose to. He went outside and began kicking a ball around the yard as though that might help.

It was difficult for him, she knew, she had kept him outside of things which mattered to her. Twins had good instincts, so in a way she was glad that Luke didn't know what was happening.

Perhaps in time she and Luke would be as close again as they had been before they left London. Things had never been quite right since then and she regretted the things that she had lost. She didn't regret her father any more. She would never forgive him for what he had done.

Cal watched Danny carefully. He looked as though he had got drunk that first night but that was understandable, Cal thought. The second day he looked tired and by the third day he was making mistakes.

Cal called him into the office and blithely said that he was hoping Danny would consider night school and Danny stood there, angry and defiant, staring out of the window, looking so much like Jaime that Cal had difficulty in remembering what he was trying to say.

'Danny, look, I know what's going on.'

He had finally caught Danny's attention.

'And is that why you want me here, because your brother's dead? You don't understand at all. I care about my dad.' His voice broke and he stopped.

'I know you do.'

'When he finds out he won't want me any more.'

'You don't know that.'

'Would you?'

'I don't have a child. It's difficult for me to imagine.'

'My dad is going to go mad like nobody else ever did and then… I'm not going to no night school,' Danny said and he went back to work.

'Is there summat up with our Danny?'

Jessie had been dreading the words for days. Now that her husband had finally uttered them, she turned trembling hands away from the table she was laying and turned around. It was Sunday afternoon.

Keir always went to the pub at dinner time, came back, had his dinner and then went to bed to sleep it off before the evening session.

She had never before now been thankful for his addiction to beer, but she had been since Danny had been told of his parentage because she thought that Keir might not notice. It had been a vain hope; even with work during the week, the pub every night and twice on Sundays, Keir knew that something was wrong.

He did not often question her about the children but she had worried because Danny was not himself, he was unhappy like he had not been before and it was obvious, at least to her.

'I think he's had a falling out with some lass he was keen on,' she said.

Keir stared. 'Our Danny's got a lass?'

'I don't know,' she said.

Danny came in at that point. He had been out all afternoon but it was awful timing, Jessie thought. Danny had lost weight, his face was sullen and he quite obviously didn't care about who he was nice to because he didn't speak, he walked straight through the kitchen, up the stairs. The next thing Jessie heard was the bedroom door clashing.

'What makes you think it's a lass?' Keir said.

'What else would it be, him in a mood like that?'

Keir went up the stairs after him. Jessie watched him and dreaded what might happen next.

Danny was sitting on the bed, he didn't expect his dad to come in. The room was full of beds. He thought of Luke having a bedroom all to himself in that great big house and for the first time ever envied him.

'What's up with you?' Keir said.

'Nowt.'

'It didn't sound like nowt. You didn't even speak.'

'I don't have to, do I?'

Danny knew he was on dangerous ground here, he never cheeked his dad, and it was, he thought miserably, a mark of how much Keir loved him that he didn't immediately give him the hiding that most lads would have got after a week of such behaviour.

'No, you don't have to.'

Danny listened to the silence as it went on and on. He wanted to break down and cry like a little lad and tell Keir all about it and how much he wanted him still for his dad but he couldn't.

'I'm thinking I might go and live somewhere else,' he said.

'Somewhere else?'

'Aye. There's a lass at the pub, she's got a room, she told me I could move in with her.'

'What lass? What pub?'

'The Fisherman's Arms.'

'What, that little blonde-haired thing? Half the men in the place have had her. Is that what you want?'

'Aye,' Danny looked defiantly at him. 'That's what I want. Is she supposed to be to blame for what men do?'

'No, of course she's not. It's just that...'

'It's just that what? Have you had her?'

Keir faltered and Danny knew that it was not that he had done such a thing but that Danny might accuse him of it.

'You do everything else,' Danny said. 'We've struggled on all these years while you've done nowt but booze and spend money and we've lived here in this hovel with my mam having bairns and us getting poorer. Do you think you're somebody to give me advice about my life? Well, do you? You're disgusting.'

It took Danny a minute or two to work out that what he really wanted was for Keir to hit him. He had put his dad into the kind of situation now where he couldn't win, because if he hit him it would break the bond between them and if he didn't he was the kind of man who would let himself be insulted and do nothing.

Keir went on looking at him for so long that Danny badly wanted to turn away but he made himself not, he waited for the blow that never came and finally Keir said, 'However bad it is I'll stand it, I promise.'

Danny wanted to cry so much that his face hurt.

'I've got through a lot of hard things in my life–' Keir said and Danny interrupted, shouting.

'No, you haven't,' he said, 'that's why you drink, because you cannot get past them. It's me mam that takes the weight around here, not you. You're useless. You've never got over the things your mam and dad did to you even though you've been married to me mam years and years and she's always been good and kind to you when you didn't deserve it. She deserved better than you.'

'Aye, I know she did. The trouble is, Danny, that people are what their parents made them. I don't think you get past it.'

Danny laughed. How ironic was that.

The door opened and his mam stood there.

'Will you stop shouting at your dad?' she said. 'I can hear you downstairs. You're not going to live with no barmaid. You're not going any place.'

'I'll do what I like.'

'Shut up, Danny,' she said.

'I can't go on with this no longer.'

'Danny–'

But he said it.

'You're not my dad. You're nothing to do with me and I'm nothing to do with you and I'm not standing this any more. I'm going.'

His mam was yelling at him to shut up but it was his dad who stopped him as he made for the door. It was the first time his dad had laid hands on him in anger and as Keir slammed him up against the wall Danny thought he would have had to fight hard and well to move. He was both relieved and regretted what he had said.

'Explain yourself.'

'You're not my dad.'

Keir looked at Jessie. She had put both hands over her face.

'Is this right?' he said.

She took her hands down.

'Yes.'

'There was somebody else?'

He sounded so calm, Danny thought.

'Jaime Gray.'

'Danny is Jaime Gray's?'

'Yes.'

'He wouldn't marry you?'

Danny was beginning to think that his dad's voice was going to go on like that for ever, flat and calm like an incoming tide on a clear day.

'He wanted to. I wouldn't.'

'Even though he knew about Danny?'

'I didn't love him!' She shouted it at him. 'I only did it because … because you had gone off with Thelma Smith. I didn't mean to do it. It was a mistake. He went off and married Ailsa. He ran away because he couldn't stand to be here.'

'You went with him because I took Thelma Smith to a dance?'

Keir was right, Danny thought, it sounded really daft.

'I didn't…' She looked at Danny and then down at her feet. 'He made me do it.'

'What, he forced you?'

'No. No, he … he just … kept on doing things to me until I gave in. It's not the same thing. You know it isn't. You've done that plenty of times.'

Danny would have got out of the room if there had been any way in which he could have but Keir had one arm across him, effectively holding him hard against the wall. If anything, that arm had increased in pressure as the conversation went on and Danny was frightened now, he could feel his heart beating.

'You let me think Danny was mine so that we got married.'

'I loved you!'

The silence was awful and after it Danny could hear Shannon bringing the bairns back with the shopping. They were all talking at once, their voices flowed up through the ceiling, light, joyous, ready for their tea.

'So why now?' Keir said and really, Danny thought, he was the only one of them who was thinking properly.

'Because of Margaret Gray,' Danny said. 'I've been…' He realized as he said it that nothing had actually happened and in fact, like adults always did, they were fussing on about nothing.

Or were they? Where might it have led had it been left to grow and develop? Might he and Margaret have fallen in love or would some instinct better in her than it was in him save them from irreparable mistakes?

'She's the lass?'

'Yes.'

'So Ailsa Gray and – and Callum, they know all about this? I'm the only one who didn't know.'

'Well, you know now,' Jessie said and the tears were running down her face.

'When were you going to tell me?' he said, looking at her.

'Never.'

'Like you never did before?'

'Like that. I didn't want to hurt you.'

Keir said nothing. It was the very opposite of the way in which Danny had thought his dad would react. He couldn't think why now. Keir was not given to shouting. The very absence of his voice was something Danny remembered back through the years. He had never shouted at them. He had never, so far as Danny knew, shouted at anybody.

He had knocked the shit out of people of course but not at home and his quietness was in part an admission of his very serious faults. His dad knew who he was and knew also that he could not change who he was because he could not survive without the beer, he could not manage being the person he was, looking at himself coldly and living.

There had been two other things which had propped him up, one of them had been the love Jessie had for him and the other had been how proud he was of his son. Now he had no son and Danny had no father and it was a huge loss all round, Danny thought. And she had proved unfaithful so that took care of the other bit.

Keir released him so that Danny almost fell over and then walked out without saying anything more. Jessie, the minute she heard him leave, sat down on the bed and put her face into her hands. Danny said to her, 'You shouldn't cry. It cannot be good for the baby,' and then he remembered that this was all his fault and couldn't think of anything else to say. Finally she lifted her head, as though she knew what he was thinking, and she said, 'You were right to tell him. There was never going to be a good time and it would have been worse if he'd found it out in some other way.'

Danny nodded and then he began to put together the few clothes that he possessed.

'You are going?' she said.

'Yes, I'm going. I can't stop here now.'

'You won't really go to–'

'No, I won't.'

'Where will you go, then?'

'I'll lodge with somebody.'

Jessie was old enough by now to know that what you least expected usually happened. Danny left. Keir did not refer to him again. He didn't touch her and it was literal. They lay turned away from one another in the night.

He had, before this, spent most of his time either at work or in the pub but now he came home only to wash, change, eat and sleep.

He did not speak to her or to the children other than necessities. It was almost as bad as if he had hit her, Jessie thought.

All she said to Shannon was that Danny and his dad had had a disagreement. Without Danny's wage it was almost impossible for them to live. Although she felt bad minding that Danny's wage mattered so much, it was true.

Because Keir didn't speak she couldn't even ask him to give them more money. Like the children used to, she would wait until he slept and then go through his pockets for money.

The first time they spoke was a week after Danny had gone and he accused her of emptying his pockets.

'We have to live,' she said.

'I gave you what I could at the beginning of the week. The fact that we haven't enough to live on is down to you.'

Jessie tried not to lose her temper.

'You are drinking every night.'

'If you want me to go on living here that's what I'll be doing.'

'And what about your bairns?'

'Who's to say that any of them's mine,' he said.

'That's a very low remark, Keir.'

He looked at her.

'I cannot understand why you didn't tell me.'

'Would you have married me with another lad's baby in me?'

'No, and we would both have been better off,' he said.

The following day they were having stew for tea and he complained.

'There's no meat at all in this.'

'We haven't got money for meat.'

Keir threw his plate into the fireplace. It could, Jessie thought, picking the bits up when he had slammed out of the house, have been much worse. It could have been her or the children.

'I'll do that, Mam,' Shannon said and Jessie went to comfort Theresa, who was crying. The other two children went on eating as though nothing had happened.

Later, when the children were in bed and Jessie could at last sit down, Shannon came back from reading them a story and sat down with her by the fire. They sat without talking, waiting for the evening to get itself past.

Jessie, exhausted, went to bed early. Shannon sat over the fire and her father came home early. Strangely enough he did not seem drunk. He looked at her. Shannon looked straight into his eyes. They were her own eyes.

'Is somebody going to tell me what's going on?' she said.

'You mean you don't know? I thought the whole bloody place knew that Danny was Jaime Gray's bastard.'

He said the word with such bitterness that Shannon flinched. She wanted to say, 'My mam wouldn't do such a thing,' but she could tell that it was true so she didn't.

'Thought she was perfect, did you?' Shannon said, suddenly angry.

He frowned. 'I don't know what you mean.'

'It was a mistake.'

'How do you know that?'

'Don't be soft. If she hadn't cared so much about you why would she have put up with you? You were no great catch to begin with. She always knew you were useless. Mam doesn't have any faults other than she sometimes swears when she gets cross. What entitles you to be married to somebody almost perfect when you're so hopeless? Now you've discovered she makes a mess of things—'

'He's not my son!' her dad cut in.

'You brought him up and he thinks the world of you.'

Keir turned away.

'Did you put him out?' Shannon asked softly.

'No. He told me and then he went.'

'Jaime Gray's dead. He cannot go to him.'

'They'll take him in. He's one of theirs.'

'He's one of us,' Shannon said.

'Not any more,' Keir said.

Shannon was amazed at herself. She had not realized up to that point how much she cared about Danny. She would have done anything for him and also for her mam and her dad not to fall out over it, though there was no help.

Her mam had made one mistake, her dad had made dozens and kept on repeating them over and over. Why should her mam have to pay so dearly and her dad not?

There was no justice for women and she didn't want to be a part of this conspiracy that made women keep house, have children, put up with their husband's disgusting habits and political opinions.

She knew how endearing her father could be but he was breaking her mother's heart like this and it was not a dramatic thing to think, he was hurting her badly and Shannon could not bear it.

Her mam put up with her dad's serious faults, yet he could not bear that she had done something wrong. She would stand by her mam always, even if it meant giving up her dream of being a nun, of giving herself to God. She was beginning to think that if God was made in man's image he did not deserve women.

The following day was Saturday. Shannon went to see Margaret. She marched up to the front door and asked for her straight out and Margaret came to the door and outside.

'Where's our Danny?'

'I don't know. I haven't seen him. Don't you know where he is?'

'He left our house after he had a row with my dad. I thought maybe he was at yours.'

Margaret shook her head.

Shannon asked all over the village. She no longer cared what people thought or that she invited curious looks, she just wanted to find where he was and eventually located him. He was lodging with an old lady who let rooms on the front street.

It was all right, Shannon thought, being ushered up steep stairs, and when she banged on the door indicated Danny opened it. He stood back and let her in.

It was a nice room, Shannon decided, big and high, and it had a window which looked out over the sea. It was clean and tidy but then Danny had no possessions, nothing but a few shabby clothes, so he could hardly make a mess.

'You could have told me where you were,' she said, looking at him. She thought he looked dreadful, like somebody ill.

'Didn't want to,' Danny said, subsiding on to the bed. 'How's Mam?'

Shannon wanted to say something encouraging but she couldn't tell lies so she just shook her head.

'And – and him?'

'He's worse than ever.'

'Well, he would be, wouldn't he?'

'I cannot understand why women like me mam marry men like me dad,' Shannon said. 'He's just a big good-looking nowt.'

'I thought he might have done summat worse.'

'He'd be hard pushed to be any worse,' she said and won a smile from Danny.

'Here,' he said, taking money from his pocket and giving it to her.

'I can't take it.'

'If you come by every week I'll give you some more,' Danny said. 'I don't need it. I get all my meals here and Mr Gray is paying for me to go to night school.'

'I thought you didn't want to go.'

'There's nowt else to do,' Danny said. 'Take it.'

Shannon didn't know what to say, she had never seen him so upset. She couldn't even tell him that she wanted him to come back, or that her dad wanted him there, but to leave Danny here in this room by himself seemed such an awful thing to do.

'I'm sorry,' she said.

'Aye, I'm sorry too,' he said. 'Shouldn't you get back?'

'Mam's all on her own.'

'Well, then,' Danny said and since she couldn't think of anything more to say that might help, Shannon walked back through the town and up the steep hill towards home.

Keir ignored Danny at work but it was a small business, only a hundred men, so it was difficult not to see him several times a day.

In some ways it was comforting because he had always loved Danny so much that not to see him a lot was a burden but knowing Danny was not his son, his only son, sat with him like a bad meal all the time. He could not understand why Jaime Gray, a stupid bugger like him, could be given two sons and other people should not have any.

He wasn't sure whether Cal Gray looked after Danny better now he knew who he was or whether he had intended all along to try and turn Danny into a manager.

Either way Cal kept Danny close to him and it seemed to Keir that he was going to have the almost impossible task of being managed by a lad he had spent sixteen years thinking was his and that Cal was obliged to do this. The other lad, Luke, had no desire to have anything to do with foundries whereas it was obvious to everybody in the place that Danny took to it as was bred in him.

Keir knew, through talk, that Cal had insisted on Danny going to night school and Keir thought that he was quite right, you had to have education if you were going to run things. He couldn't help being proud of Danny right before the sick feeling of remembering Danny was nothing to do with him any more but then he felt the same at home.

He couldn't bring himself to speak to

Jessie. He knew it was very small-minded considering he had been such an awful husband to her but pretending to forgive somebody and being able to do it were two different things. He didn't want to be there and worst of all, in some ways, he couldn't get the beer down. He didn't understand why that was.

It had something to do with the fact that Danny almost always came and collected him and it had been the best time of the day somehow.

Knowing that he would have to go home alone and not via the beach and not in Danny's company made it worthless and that was funny. He had always thought it was the beer he wanted but it was not, it was the underlying joy of Danny's presence in his life. Without that he wanted nothing.

His change of habits was not lost on his wife and he did not miss the look of surprise on her face when he began to come home from work and not go to the pub. He went out, he walked and tried to talk to himself in an attempt to make some sense of what had happened, but the missing of Danny was a huge ache, such as nothing before. He felt as if his son had died.

His friends did not seem to comprehend

what had happened. Keir couldn't understand this. Usually, once a secret got out, everybody knew but this secret was so well contained that nobody talked about it.

People just thought he and Danny had had a disagreement, which was usual with men and their sons, and that Danny had left because he was almost grown up and because they had fallen out.

Keir longed to say that he could never disagree with Danny like that but he couldn't. He had to leave it. They were ready to accept that he temporarily didn't want their company because of it so he began to go home in the evenings and then drive himself mad, sitting about while Jessie conducted the affairs of the house and the girls did what they usually did.

He and Jessie didn't talk and Shannon wouldn't speak to him so coming home was not good and the lack of beer, company and Danny meant that Keir was more unhappy than he had ever been. In fact he had not known how happy he had been until now when it was all taken away. There was, however, one good side.

The first Friday afternoon he went home and tipped up the whole of his pay to Jessie. She stared. He put the wage packet into her hand unopened. Keir didn't give her time to say anything, he banged out of the house.

She looked just as surprised the following week when he did the same, because she obviously didn't expect it. On the third occasion she put herself in front of him – she was getting quite big by now with the baby so it would have been very bad indeed to try and shift her forcibly – and she said, 'Are we going to go on like this for always?'

'Would you rather I moved out?'

'I would rather you remembered you have four bairns and not ignore them like you're doing. You're their dad, they care about you but they don't seem to matter to you because they're lasses. What sort of an impression does that make on them, do you think?'

'I don't know.'

'Well, you should know. And if you think any of them aren't yours–'

'I didn't mean that.'

'No, well, you just have to look at them to see they're yours. I'm sorry for what I did, Keir, I know you're heartbroken about Danny–'

'You don't understand. It's all right for you, you know he's yours.'

'You brought him up and he cares about

you. What must he think?'

'Oh, he's all right. Cal Gray treats him like one of the family at work. Danny will have the foundry one day and I'll be calling him "Mister".'

'And what's wrong with that?' she said.

Keir didn't answer and Jessie faltered.

'I didn't mean it like that,' she said.

That night she tried to put her arms around him in bed and he was obliged to shake her off without doing any damage. The trouble was, he thought, the damage was all done.

It had not occurred to Luke that he could dislike Danny. They hardly ever saw each other any more and he resented that he had lost the friendship which mattered so much to him.

He hadn't thought at first that it did, he wasn't given to making friends. Margaret had always been enough until Danny.

Now it seemed as though Danny had come between them, firstly by making up to Margaret and then by being accepted into the works and even given a space and a desk in the main office. Luke thought that was strange and questioned his uncle about it.

'You can come into the foundry if you

like,' Cal said. 'I didn't think you wanted to.'

'I don't,' Luke said, frustrated and then realized he was jealous. Cal didn't talk about work at home so Danny's name never passed his lips and Margaret, for all the brave talk, was obviously very upset about Danny's having left her. Because that's what he had done, Luke could tell.

He was angry on her behalf, but when he questioned her all she would say was that she never wanted to see Danny again as long as she lived. That was hardly the same as her offhand way of saying earlier that Danny had gone off with somebody else and she didn't care.

Luke discovered that Danny had left home. He went to the house and found Shannon, awkward, at the back door.

'Is Danny in?' It was Sunday afternoon, their traditional time for getting together, so he should have been.

'No,' Shannon said.

'He can't be at work.'

'I don't know where he is.'

Luke looked at her in such a way that Shannon said, 'Me dad's in.'

That was a surprise. It was early afternoon and Keir was always at the pub, but there he was, behind her in the doorway, looking more sober and darker than Luke could remember. He said, 'What do you want?' in a way that would have cowed just about anybody.

'I just wanted to see Danny.'

'Danny's not here any more,' Keir said and he drew his daughter inside and shut the door.

Danny felt that it shouldn't have been any surprise that the landlord of the Black Diamond came to him at his lodgings on a Sunday a month after he had moved out of the house. He stood apologetically in the hallway outside Danny's room and said, 'Can you come and get your dad?'

Danny wanted to say that Keir wasn't his dad and therefore, no, he wouldn't, but he couldn't because other people, for some reason, didn't know. And he didn't want them to know so he put on his jacket and went.

How odd that he felt homesickness when he walked in at the door of the pub. The smell of beer, cigarettes and the smoking fire made him think of how he never saw Keir home any more. Bill was right, he had never seen Keir so drunk. He was unconscious, lying on the floor by the fire.

'We tried to move him,' Bill said, 'but we couldn't. It's the first time he's been in since you left. Practically drank the place dry. And he hasn't paid for it.'

'How much?'

Bill named the sum. Danny put the money on the bar top and then got down beside Keir and he thought he had never loved his dad so much. How stupid. Keir looked so vulnerable lying there and so young, not like he had a wife and four children, more like a boy who couldn't manage his life any more. Danny knew exactly how that felt.

'Hey, are you coming home?' he said.

There was no reply and after another go Danny was rather inclined to say to Bill that he thought he should go for the doctor when Keir opened his eyes and said, in his beautiful, Londonderry voice, 'Why, Danny, whatever are you doing here?' just as though there was nothing the matter.

'I've come to collect you,' Danny said.

Keir sat up, looking around in a surprised fashion and then he said, 'Ah, you needn't have bothered. I can see myself home.' He eyed Bill. 'You'll make somebody a lovely mother,' he said and got neatly to his feet and left the building.

'It's all right, Bill,' Danny said as Bill

began to explain and he hurried out.

He caught up with Keir before he turned the corner which would take him in the opposite direction to the beach and he said, 'Aren't you going to the sands, then?'

'What would I want to do that for?'

'We always do.'

Keir stopped.

'Did,' he said.

'It wasn't my fault,' Danny said.

'Is somebody blaming you?'

'Aye, you are, you bastard,' Danny said. He thought it was no wonder Keir looked shocked and said, without thinking, 'If you weren't...' and then stopped.

'If I weren't what? I'm living on me own in the one room at Mrs O'Connor's because you won't have me in your house any more, that's how much you think it's my fault–'

'I didn't put you out, you left.'

'You were always my dad,' Danny went on anyway. 'Now I haven't got one and you have no more sense than to try and drown yourself in beer, you useless bugger!' Danny ran away, pausing halfway down the street and turning back to say, 'And you owe me, an' all. I've just paid your bloody bar bill.' Then he ran upstairs into the room which was the only home he had left and clashed

191

the door and he stood behind it, breathing hard and not crying.

There was to be little respite. Only an hour went by before there was another knock on the door. Danny opened it to find Luke standing there.

'I went to your house the other day and your dad said you'd left,' Luke said when Danny let him in. 'What the hell's going on?'

'Me dad put me out.' Danny couldn't look at him and certainly couldn't tell him the truth.

'Why?'

'I went with the barmaid at the Fisherman's Arms. She asked me to move in with her.'

Luke stared. 'But you're here,' he said. 'On your own.'

Danny couldn't dispute that. 'I changed me mind like,' he said.

Luke shifted for a minute or two, walking about the room as though fascinated by it. Then he said, looking straight at Danny, 'I don't believe you.'

Danny gave a helpless grin. This should be getting easier by now but it wasn't.

'Why are you telling me a lie?'

Danny had always liked Luke but he had

never thought Luke very clever. Now he revised this opinion.

'There must be a good reason for it,' Luke said. 'Margaret keeps saying she doesn't want to see you and you say it's a barmaid but I don't think it's like that.

'Margaret's really upset about this and so is my mother and nobody's saying anything. So are you going to tell me what's going on or shall I go to my uncle about it, because he's involved too. I'm the only one who doesn't know.'

'Hardly anybody knows,' Danny said.

'Who else?'

'My mam and ... and my dad and our Shannon.'

'In other words everybody except Grandma and me. Why am I left out?'

Luke was starting to sound resentful and bad-tempered as though the knowledge was some kind of Christmas treat. Danny recalled some saying or other, 'Ignorance is bliss, 'tis folly to be wise'. That was certainly true in this case.

'It isn't summat anybody would want to know unless they had to,' Danny said.

'Nevertheless I think you should tell me,' Luke said sounding impressively grown up.

'All right. My mam...' This should be

getting easier with all the telling, only it wasn't. 'My mam and your dad, they had a thing going and I was the result.'

Luke stared at him. Danny waited.

'That's not true,' Luke said.

'It is.'

'My father would never have done such a thing. Your mother is a liar!' Luke said and he ran out.

Luke practically fell into Margaret's bedroom. She looked up in surprise at the way that he burst in.

'Is this true?' he said. 'Danny is Dad's?'

It was not the way that Margaret would have chosen to explain what had happened but it was, she had to agree, the truth.

'Yes, it's right,' she said.

'Why didn't you tell me? We always tell each other everything.'

'Not since Danny,' Margaret said.

Luke collapsed on to the bed. He had been running hard and was out of breath. He stared up at the ceiling. Somehow it had never occurred to him that Danny was getting in the way of his close relationship with his twin.

It had always been the two of them against the rest of mankind and more special than anything else, everybody else always on the outside, and he was upset and jealous.

He liked Danny up to a point but he and Margaret had been more than that, he had very often known what she was thinking, what she would say. If they were apart he knew when she wanted to talk to him, when she was upset, needy. He felt so left out, so alone like never before.

'And that's what happened? Because of you and Danny?'

'Yes.'

Luke turned over on to his front and began picking out the swirling patterns on the bedstead with his fingers. He said, 'Why didn't I understand any of this? I used to know things without you explaining. Since we've come here everything's gone wrong.'

'Things had gone wrong long since,' Margaret said.

'Yes, but not between you and me. It's all altered.'

Margaret didn't say anything to that. Luke turned over again and stared at the watermarks on the ceiling.

'It's the kind of thing Dad would do.'

Margaret sighed as if a weight had lifted, as though she was not the only person still holding up the world.

'Yes.'

'He didn't really like us.'

'No, he didn't.'

'Do you think he would have liked Danny?'

'I think he would have hated Danny,' she said.

'Did you know Danny had left home? His … Mr Logan put him out and he's lodging on the front street. It must be awful. Parents. They're no bloody good at all.'

'What about Mother?'

'She's pathetic,' Luke said. 'I don't know what she married him for.'

'She must have loved him in the beginning.'

'Huh,' Luke said and then he went on awkwardly, 'I don't want us to stop being friends with Danny and Shannon, no matter how things are.'

'Neither do I,' Margaret said.

Twelve

Ailsa had been thinking about the piano. It was a baby grand and polished to a high shine but unused. She tried to ignore the way she was drawn to it.

The door was always closed so it should not have been a temptation, but she could not help going inside and looking at it every day, afraid to put her hands on the keys, her fingers were so stiff, she had not played for years, and remembering how much Jaime had hated her playing. Somehow every time she went near it she was reminded of her unhappy marriage.

Beethoven, Bach and Jaime. How awful. How stupid, she told herself, yet she did not seem capable of sitting down on the green-velvet-topped stool and looking through the great pile of music which lay on top of the piano.

And then one day early that autumn she came back from doing some shopping to find the door of the music room open and sounds coming from the piano, not the sounds of somebody playing, just notes, the same ones again and again. She was afraid that somebody was in there who shouldn't be, who wouldn't treat a piano as it should be treated and when she reached the open door an oldish man, white-haired, was standing in front of it, obviously tuning it.

'What are you doing that for?' she asked.

He looked at her.

'So it sounds in tune,' he said, rather taken aback at her obvious question.

'But nobody plays it.'

'That's nothing to do with me. Mr Gray, he asked me to come and tune it. It's better for the piano that way.'

Cal, interfering, she thought with some warmth and turned around and walked away. Yet he had not mentioned it. Was he going to make some silly suggestion, such as that the children should learn to play?

Neither of them was musical. They took after Jaime that way. He had hated music and because of that she had not been able to instil any love into the children, even though it had been important and she would have liked to.

That evening, when Cal came home, she said to him over supper, 'Why is the piano being tuned?'

He looked at her as though she was asking a really stupid question.

'It's done every six months or so.'

'But nobody plays it.'

He looked nonplussed.

'Well, it's still a good piano and I like things to work.'

'Nobody goes in the music room except you and me in the evenings.'

'No, but … it's looked after, it's part of the house and I like sitting there late at night by the fire.'

'I didn't know that.'

'No, well, you're welcome to stay late there if you want to.'

He wouldn't have said this had they not been alone, she thought but the children had eaten earlier and disappeared. She hated to think what they were doing.

His mother ate earlier too and very often now in the evenings there was just the two of them and the cook had taken to asking her if there was anything she particularly fancied for supper and she would try to make it.

Ailsa had not thought she would have been pleased with the cook but it was a slight conspiracy. Mrs Pierce was the kind of woman who, though well aware of the shortages, considered the whole thing a challenge and began producing things like partridge or pheasant of a Saturday night when the children had trays in their room and Cal's mother went off to meet her friends.

The last Saturday in October Mrs Pierce excelled herself with chicken in butter, potatoes from the garden and various vegetables and then a cream and egg dessert and Cal said since Mrs Pierce was obviously going to a lot of trouble they deserved wine.

He went down mysteriously to the cellar and came back with something which tasted suspiciously of gooseberries very cold, and then a red wine which was like blackberries but thicker and better. The trouble was that Ailsa was not used to wine and began to feel extremely pleased with life when she had had a glass and slightly more of both. She was emboldened to say, 'Would you object if I was to play the piano?'

They were sitting over the fire and it was cosy. He said, 'We never have music.'

'Do you like music?'

'Yes, of course,' he said, as though it was most natural thing in the world.

'I don't mean now.'

'So when do you mean?'

'When I've practised.'

'Next Saturday, then.'

She laughed.

'Cal, I haven't played much in years. It will take months before I'm fit to be heard.'

'Oh, please,' he said, 'I would love to hear you.'

Cal very often went over to the vicarage on Friday and Saturday nights because even though he was working most of the week he liked to give himself the illusion of having time off but it was very unsatisfactory.

He was never alone with Phoebe. Her parents seemed to have lost whatever tact they had and even though the vicarage was an extremely large house and he made sure they had plenty of coal, there was never more than one fire lit and the weather was never warm enough somehow to penetrate the thick stone walls of the building.

Huddling over the fire while Mr Wilson made small talk and his wife knitted was not Cal's idea of a pleasant evening during his small amount of time off. He thought he might as well be at home doing paperwork.

He suggested to Phoebe that they should go to a dance which was being held in the Mechanics' Institute. She stared at him.

'Won't the men from the foundry be there?'

'Shouldn't think so. Most of them are married. We could be the only older people there.' It was meant to be a joke. Phoebe stared at him and then smiled.

That Saturday Cal found himself reluctant. The children were out – he had stopped asking them where they went because they seemed to feel an obligation to lie to him – his mother had gone to a birthday party for an old friend and Ailsa was alone. Cal felt guilty about leaving her there by herself. It seemed a grim thing to do to anybody on a Saturday night.

'I shall be glad of the peace,' she said, smiling and then, 'Oh, I didn't mean to imply–'

'I know. Try not to worry about the twins. I'm sure they can take care of themselves. They'll probably let you get halfway through the evening and then come in with a lot of noise.'

The opposite, as he was certain she knew, was right. They sneaked about so that most of the time nobody knew where they were.

'You go and have a lovely time. Give my best to Phoebe.'

Cal went. It was a cool October night. Little piles of leaves lay in the gutters. Phoebe was waiting for him and for once she was wearing a pretty dress. They walked through the streets to the Mechanics' Institute.

Unfortunately, Cal thought, when they got there, he was right. Other people their age were married and most men were either in uniform or their wives were at home and they were away, fighting, so it was not the right kind of place for him to be with Phoebe.

Also as he walked in he could see the twins with Shannon and Danny. Cal groaned inwardly. Was there no getting away from people?

Luke was facing the door. He stared for a second and then said, 'Oh, no,' and turned around to the others.

'What?' Danny said.

'Uncle bloody Cal.'

'What in the hell is he doing here?' Margaret said.

They huddled closer together.

'Has he seen us?' Shannon said softly.

'Of course. He's not blind.'

'Well, we aren't doing anything,' Shannon said.

'Is he coming over?' Luke said.

Danny, facing the door, kept his gaze steady.

'No,' he said at length. 'He's gone into the other room.'

'You don't think they're going to dance, do you?' Margaret said. 'We would have to leave, I couldn't stomach it.'

'Let's go anyway,' Danny said.

'No, we've paid. Besides, I've never danced with Shannon,' Luke said.

'You didn't ask,' Shannon said.

'Oh, go on. You won't get to dance with me when you're a nun, you know.'

They went off. Danny looked at Margaret.

'Well, we can't dance with each other, can we?'

'Not very well. Let's go and get a drink, if we can avoid Uncle Cal.'

Shannon liked dancing with Luke, which surprised her. He was graceful and didn't try to put his hands all over her like some boys had done in the past, but then you couldn't do that with friends or you would lose the friendship. And Luke wasn't very good at making friends and she was always too busy so they would have to stick with each other.

'We should go back,' she said when the music ended.

'Not yet.'

'Danny and Margaret are still where we

left them.'

'They can dance with other people if they want to.'

So she gave in and danced again.

'Do you like me better these days?' he said.

'You're all right.'

'You prefer God, though?'

'You're not funny,' Shannon said.

'Hasn't it occurred to you that being a nun might be dull?'

'It can't be worse than looking after small children all day. I have no intention of doing what my mother did. She made a mess of her life and got landed with my dad and all of us. What kind of an existence is that?'

'It's all most women want.'

'That isn't true and only a man would think it.'

'You don't want to marry me, then?'

He looked so comical that Shannon started to laugh.

Shannon went to church the following day, just to test herself, she had really enjoyed being with Luke and was slightly worried that she was wrong about herself.

She liked going. If she had had nothing else to do she would have gone to mass every day, it was so peaceful there, the big echoing because the ceiling was so high and it seemed so luxurious with the statues in red and gold.

She felt as though God was in the church and that was the most important thing about it, when she was there she felt as though she could let Him take care of everything and that it would be all right.

When she got home again she would think the feeling of security was an illusion but when she was in the church it seemed to her more real than anything else in her life.

She had heard that nuns' lives were hard but it did not seem to her that it would be hard, to get up early and pray, to sing with other women, to live simply and for God.

She was living in a hard way now, all her efforts went into working at the Wilsons' and helping her mother with the children and it was not something she thought she would ever want for herself. It seemed so pointless. The love of the children was very nice but it was nothing compared to the love of God.

She wanted more than anything in the world to be away from that shabby little house and not to have to think about what she would wear or how she would make the money go further, or the awful mundane jobs such as dealing with crying babies, dirty nappies and the mess her parents had made of everything.

She had thought she could forgive them anything. She could not forgive them what had happened to Danny. She missed him. She wished she could have left home too. Anywhere other than here would have done.

When she asked Father Keeley about becoming a nun he smiled and said that she must know her own mind well before she could take such steps. She did not want him to think her impatient so she said nothing more, but in a way she felt as though he had taken from her a last hope of escape. If she had to wait much longer to get away she thought she would die.

Danny would have given her more money if she had gone to his lodgings and asked, but she did not like to and there was no way in which they would meet any more except with Margaret and Luke.

She was always at home or at the Wilsons' and Danny was always at the works or the house where he lived. She never saw him in the street because he was at the foundry. The only time she went out apart from church was to do the shopping, and even then she had to take the children with her unless they were at school.

The nights were drawing in, the days were colder and that meant more coal for the fires, as much hot food as they could afford for the children and the threat of Christmas.

Christmas was Shannon's favourite time of the year except for Easter, because it was Jesus's birthday and she loved the holy things connected with it, but they never had any extra money at Christmas and this year her mother would have another baby by then. Shannon did not know whether she could stand the weight of another child.

Her father had stopped going to the pub almost altogether, to her surprise, so there was more money but without Danny's wage and with the extra child and the cold weather they would barely have enough to live on and could she keep working and leave her mam alone with four small children?

Also Keir was not a pleasure to have around the house. He barely spoke and her mother had no time for conversation. Meals were eaten in silence except for correcting the children and saying things like, 'Pass the salt, please,' so she had come to dread them. Her father would sit sideways at the table as though he longed to be somewhere else or was about to get up and walk out.

Sometimes she thought he did not even notice they were there, sometimes she thought he didn't know where he was or care, so they had that in common. She longed for some privacy, some space, some silence. One dark night after supper that November she had had enough and made for the door only to find her father for once attending and he said, 'Where do you think you're going?'

'Out.'

'No, you're not.'

Shannon, with boots, coat and scarf on, looked into the shadows of the outside door. She turned.

'Why can't I?'

'Because it's late, dark, cold and half the village will be drunk.'

'You would know,' she said.

'I would, yes.'

'You used to let our Danny out. Just because I'm a girl–'

'Just because you're a girl would be the very reason some of those lads wouldn't think twice about forcing you to do things you would have no intention of doing. Don't be daft.'

'Will you come with me, then?'

He seemed surprised at the question. She knew very well that he didn't go because the pub was too big a temptation.

'You and Danny used to walk back from the pub every night,' she said. 'I never got to.'

'I don't think the Black Diamond was terribly suitable for you,' he said with a sliver of humour.

'Some lasses go into pubs. They serve behind bars.'

'You're not going to,' he said. 'I thought you had other ideas.'

'I just want to get away from the bairns for a few minutes. Is that such a lot to ask?'

'All right,' he said. He took down his jacket and his cap from the nail where they hung and shouted back into the kitchen, 'Jessie, I'm taking our Shannon out for a few minutes.' Like she was a dog, Shannon thought, wanting to slam the door either after or before him.

The stupid part about it was that it was actually a big novelty to be outside in the cold when it was dark, and especially with her dad who never invited her to do anything.

'Shall we go to the beach?'

'No,' he said.

'You used to go with our Danny to the beach, he told me once.'

'That's why,' Keir said.

They walked along the main street and he was right, she could never have done this on her own. Outside the Miners' Arms two lads were fighting and a dozen were egging them on, yelling, and some of it wasn't fit for hearing. Further along at another of the pubs there was singing and a big gang of lads outside.

Keir had his hands in his pockets and boldly, because he never touched any of his children, she put her arm through his arm. He slowed down and looked at her and smiled and somebody said, 'Has thoo been gettin' thyself a lass, then, Keir?' Just as though he didn't have a wife and several children, Shannon thought, enraged.

Keir stopped at the three men in front of him across the pavement, not that they were threatening but he said, 'This is my daughter Shannon.'

They stared, obviously unaware that he had daughters, or at least a daughter as old as that.

'Well, by damn,' the man said, 'and isn't she the bonny one? I wish I was twenty.'

'It wouldn't do thoo no good even if thoo was, Jackie lad,' another of them said, 'she's like a film star.'

Shannon could not help smiling and the men went on standing there, the admiration shining from their eyes. Keir guided her past.

'Drunk,' he observed with all the sanctimony of somebody trying to give up.

'Thanks, Dad.'

'What?' He looked at her.

'People don't have to be drunk to think lasses are bonny.'

'Why don't we go to the beach?' Keir said as though desperate to change the subject, so they did.

The tide, Shannon thought, never disappointed you, there it was going at breakneck speed, chucking itself up the beach in good winter style, crashing and making as much noise as it could and filling the whole of her vision with movement. It was a cold night so there was a moon beyond the horizon and endless stars.

'You forget how beautiful it is when you don't see it often,' she said.

When he didn't speak she said, 'I think I might want to be a nun.'

'Aye, I know.'

'You don't mind, then?'

'Not if it's what you want.'

'You don't think, like other daft fellas, that it's a waste of a good woman.'

'There are other ways to waste a good woman,' he said. 'Plenty of them.'

Shannon felt rather strange now that she had her dad's permission, almost as though she might not want it any more because nobody was trying to stop her.

It was silly but that was how it felt. But she was grateful to him as well for not telling her what she could and what she could not do, like a lot of fathers did with their children and especially with their daughters, as though they weren't right in the head and couldn't make their own decisions. In some ways, she thought, Keir was a good dad, but only in some ways.

It panicked her to think that she might not want to be a nun when she had been so sure it was the right thing for her to do. Maybe lots of people weren't sure but went ahead with it anyway.

'Will you sing me "The Londonderry Air"?'

'No.'

'Aw, go on. You never sing anything for me and you've got such a nice voice. Go on,

Dad, sing it.'

So he did, steadily all the way through, just as Danny had reported him doing in a slow clear voice. After that they walked slowly up the beach and he took her to the most respectable pub in the place where all the businessmen and the farmers went, the White Bull on the edge of the village.

Shannon was very impressed, it had thick carpets and a big fire. He sat her down at a small round table while he went to the bar and she watched the people around her talking and the lights were low and he came back with something that she had never seen before.

'It's a snowball,' he said.

'It doesn't look like a drink.'

'Try it.'

She did. It tasted like a pudding with a kick in it, like lemon trifle. She beamed across the table at him, knowing she should not be drinking, and she was proud of him when he had one pint and then said to her, 'Shall we go home? Your mam'll think we've got lost.'

'Did you used to bring her to places like this?'

'Aye, sometimes.'

'It's nice,' Shannon said.

They walked back home with her hand through his arm and when they got there, for once the place was completely quiet. Her mam came to the door.

'Where've you been?'

'To the beach,' Shannon said.

'And the pub,' he said.

'I had a snowball.'

'Eh, there's no holding you, is there?' her mam said.

When Shannon had gone to bed Keir lingered over the fire.

'Aren't you coming to bed?' Jessie said at last.

'No.'

He needed a drink, she knew he did. He had never in all his life had one drink and come home. If she left him there the chances were he would go back to the pub. It was not late but she was tired. The pubs were still open. She went and sat down on the little stool across the fire from him. When he didn't speak or say anything she got up and put one arm around his neck and kissed him.

'It as nice of you to take our Shannon out.'

He still didn't say anything.

'Are you never going to come to me any

more?' she said.

Nothing.

'And am I too big for you to fancy me?'

'You're too big to sit on the floor.'

'Aye, I know,' she said as he got up and she attempted to. 'Give us a hand.'

He reached out like she was a child with his hands under her arms and picked her off the floor like she weighed nothing. It had always been one of the most attractive things about him, she thought, that he could do so if he chose.

She didn't ask anything more of him, she went to bed. If he wanted the drink so badly as he had always done there was nothing she could do about it.

But he didn't go. She didn't have to lie there and listen to the door clash and then the empty sound of his not being there. He followed her slowly up the stairs. Nobody said anything. They undressed and got into bed and he turned his back.

Jessie waited until she thought he was asleep and then she put an arm around him and snuggled in against him but it was too uncomfortable for long, she knew.

After the comfort there was the discomfort of her enormous belly and she had to turn back and rearrange the pillows. Even then, the way that the baby was moving about she would be lucky to get any sleep.

The last few weeks was always like this. The difference was that he had never shut her out before when she was pregnant. She prayed and prayed to the Blessed Virgin to give her a boy. If she had a boy she would get her husband back, she knew it.

Thirteen

Ailsa couldn't get herself to the piano. She imagined herself there, she even thought of all the pieces she would play when she got there, but somehow it just didn't happen. She could always think of something else to do, a dozen things before she got to the piano. By the time she really thought she should play she had justified her entire day to herself or talked herself out of it.

After all, what was the point? She was not going to be a professional pianist and nobody with any kind of ear would want to listen to her stumblings and mistakes, so she left the piano to itself to the point where she couldn't even go into the room, she felt guilty as though it were a neglected child.

But the idea of Cal sitting night after night over the fire put her off. She did not want to be alone with him, she did not want to have to make conversation. It was too difficult and she had nothing to say to him.

He didn't press her, he didn't ask again. They went on eating dinner together and afterwards she would make an excuse and go upstairs to her room to take refuge. Cal even seemed relieved.

But the more Ailsa tried not to think about playing the piano the more she thought about it. Somehow the door was always open and on sunshiny afternoons her mother-in-law insisted on having the thick velvet curtains closed so that the sheen on the piano would not fade.

It was kept polished to a high shine. The lid was always closed and it seemed to her that the room was particularly silent.

She could not help thinking that after so many years with stiffened fingers she would only make a fool of herself. But then she thought you could grow impatient of your inadequacies but in order to make a fool of yourself you had to have another person there.

In the end, one afternoon, the house was empty. The children were at school, Cal was at work, Mrs Pierce had half a day off and his mother had gone to do some shopping.

All alone, Ailsa realized why she had turned down the invitation to go with her mother-in-law. She had wanted, subconsciously known, that she would be here alone with the piano.

It was, she thought, sliding into the room, closing the door softly even though there was no one in the house, running her fingers over the top of the instrument, the only real lover she had ever known.

She lifted the lid, looked at the keys, opened the green velvet top of the piano stool. There was a stack of music which she recognized as her own, which she had brought with her when she married and which Jaime had not encouraged her to take to London. These were the pieces which she had learned to play in the days of her mother's last illness.

In a way she had played to shut out that illness for both of them. Her mother had loved to hear and in the end she lay downstairs in that room with her eyes closed while Ailsa played all her favourite music. Here it was, Czerny, Beethoven, Bach, Burmüller, Duvernoy, Loeschhorn, Bertini, Köhler, Heller, Lemoine, Chopin, Mozart, Schubert, Clementi.

The white covers of the music collections trembled in her hands. Old friends, favourites, the music she had had by heart. And the great big grey book with the red writing which had been the most important of all, scales.

She must start with these. She opened the book at C which was the first and easiest and began with that. She played it perfectly twice and then, just as she was growing in confidence, her fingers began to stumble.

After that, as she tried harder she could play nothing until, almost in tears, she turned to a piece she had loved well. It was by Bergmüller and was entitled 'L'Harmonie des Anges'.

She played it all the way through, very badly, but she felt better when she had done it. She had been sitting there for three-quarters of an hour.

The following day her mother-in-law, the maid and Mrs Pierce were in and Ailsa hovered, going past the open door of the room several times, only giving in about an hour before Margaret and Luke were due to come back from school. After that there would be no chance of getting in there without being seen and more importantly without being heard.

She sneaked in, there was no other word for it, closing the door without a sound. She opened the piano and saw to her consternation that she had left the book of scales as though she was going to come back, propped up in full view on the front of the instrument for anybody to see.

Obviously her subconscious had known. She began to play, very softly at first. C major, minor, chromatic, harmonic, octaves, double thirds, broken chords, arpeggios, moving on to D and then G. The feel of the piano keys beneath her fingers was so exciting it made her heart want to burst.

She forgot that she had decided to keep the volume down. She forgot the time. She played again the piece she had played the day before. She made an even worse mess of it this time but somehow it didn't matter. She was perfectly happy to be there. She felt more at home than she had felt in a long time.

Every day after that she spent time in the music room, always after lunch, the time increasing until it was all afternoon. She was always finished by the time Margaret and Luke got home.

On the first Saturday evening she dreaded Cal asking her about it but evidently nobody had said anything and he didn't mention it.

By the second weekend she assumed he had forgotten. After that it was only the weekends when she did not play.

Two months went past. It was almost

Christmas and by then there was a feeling that it would not be long before the war was over. There was now lighting on buses and trains and even that small difference had ensured some kind of optimism.

It was Saturday evening. Cal's mother had taken to going out on Saturdays, to social events at the church. What Margaret and Luke did she did not like to ask. They ate early and disappeared. Somehow the routine had been established that she and Cal would eat at eight and the cook, Mrs Pierce, would do her best considering the shortages.

On Saturday afternoons Cal would take a shotgun and spend the afternoon on the fells or fields with Phoebe and come back with pheasant, partridge or duck, pigeons and even sometimes rabbit. Ailsa didn't much care for rabbit but it was not the time to complain about any food which they could gather for themselves.

They had vegetables and fruit from the garden which they had stored and Cal seemed to have a bottomless wine cellar because they always had good wine on Saturday nights.

Sometimes Phoebe came back with him but Ailsa found herself rather hoping that either he wouldn't ask her or she would refuse for some reason. She knew it wasn't very kind to wish Phoebe elsewhere but they had nothing in common, and when Phoebe did venture over on Saturday nights the conversation was strained and Ailsa would excuse herself and go to bed early. She didn't pretend to herself that Phoebe enjoyed it either, she came so seldom.

When she knew it would just be the two of them Ailsa took to dressing up. It was the only social life she had. Going out in the dark was not encouraged and since there was no money for petrol unless for business purposes, had there been anywhere interesting to go they could not have gone beyond the village.

Not that she wanted to go anywhere. Now that the dark nights were here she was happy to retreat to her bedroom with a book, since the fire was lit there every night.

Sometimes she even thought herself lucky to have escaped her loveless marriage. After half a bottle of wine on Saturday night she thought that sitting across the table from Cal and having him make decent conversation was as close as she wanted to get to a man ever again.

His conversation was very good. She had no idea why since it never seemed to be specifically about anything. They talked about the children, his mother, her memories of her mother, the friends they had known when they were young. They talked about Jaime and it was easy since there were no secrets now.

One night just before Christmas he encouraged her to sit by the fire with him, drinking brandy, and there, slightly drunk, she was emboldened to say to him, 'Why didn't you ever think about marriage until now?'

They were seated at either end of the big leather sofa and she was almost happy, full of dinner and wine and relaxed. He glanced down into his brandy glass and said, 'You broke my heart.'

She laughed. 'Nothing of the sort.'

'Yes, you did. You liked Jaime better than me.'

'Don't think I haven't regretted it. Surely you've met somebody in the last eighteen years.'

'Nobody I wanted to marry, until Phoebe.'

Ailsa didn't want to talk about Phoebe and was sorry she had invited that kind of conversation. 'Weren't you very keen on Jessie O'Brien too at one point?' she said, to change the subject.

'I certainly was. Nobody ever stood a chance with her. Jaime ought to have known.'

'Keir is … he's very attractive. Perhaps it's the idea of reform.'

Cal smiled. 'I don't think anybody will ever manage that.'

'And Danny?'

He shifted uncomfortably in his seat. 'There isn't much more I can do without looking obvious. He can't come here because of Margaret, and Keir can't have him there.'

'It seems so unfair. He's such a nice boy. Not like Jaime at all.'

'He's like Jessie. Will you play the piano for me?'

He changed the subject so suddenly that she was taken aback.

'You knew I'd been practising?'

'I've heard you from the hall now and then. It sounds good. Music is … it eases things.'

'I've had too much to drink.'

'Oh, play something. I don't care. I'm not going to be critical. I would love to hear it. We have so little music.'

'What would you like to hear?'

'Anything at all.'

Emboldened by food and wine she went to the piano. Music, she thought, was a fickle master. She played her favourite Beethoven sonata, flawlessly. After the last notes had died she went back to the fire.

'That was exquisite,' he said. 'You should have been a concert pianist.'

'You had the piano tuned on purpose.'

'No, I didn't.'

'You're such a bad liar,' she said. 'You've done so much for us.'

'It was just what anybody would have done. You and Margaret and Luke are all the family I have.'

'And Danny Logan,' she said.

Cal looked at her. He said, 'Ailsa...' and then stopped.

She was inclined to get up and run out or tell him not to do or say anything more, it would spoil things, except that there was so very little to spoil somehow. She smiled slightly and then she said, 'I made a mistake with Jaime. I shouldn't have married him. Perhaps I shouldn't have married at all. I wasn't very good at it.'

'Or he wasn't.'

'Maybe if I'd been different it would have been better and he would have forgotten Jessie. Nobody had ... had touched me before he did and I can't say I liked it much. Maybe I'm just the sort of woman who doesn't like men.'

'I thought you liked me,' he said, smiling in deliberate misunderstanding.

'I do, but that's different because you've made things easier than they might have been. It's difficult to dislike somebody who tries to help you.'

'Are you trying?'

'Not any more,' and she got up and went back to the piano.

Phoebe knew that she ought to talk her parents into going to the Grays' house for Christmas because Cal had asked after church one Sunday in December. But her father always had all kinds of people to his house on Christmas Day, a sort of open house, a party for anyone who wanted to come, and he had no intention of changing things.

'You could always pop over and see Cal later,' her mother said. They were so un-worldly, she thought, could they not see that she was losing him to his sister-in-law?

A dozen times she had tried to go to Cal's house on a Saturday evening when she knew he was alone with Ailsa and always they found something for her which had to be done. She knew it was not deliberate in them and that if she had said anything they would have told her she was being ridiculous, that of course they wanted her to spend time with Cal. But the truth was they had lost too much and could not spare her even for an hour or two.

They would never have thought of such a thing. Men did not marry their sisters-in-law, not in their respectable world. The trouble was that he didn't have to marry her, they were living in the same house and she could never think of anything to say when Ailsa was there.

It was as though Ailsa had come back to Blackhills and ruined everything.

Fourteen

Danny was dreading Christmas. It had always been the best time in their house. He had imagined that eventually he would feel better, whereas in fact he felt worse and worse. All he had now was his work and although he liked it and although Cal Gray was good to him there was nothing personal about it. He thought about the blonde girl at the pub more and more but was resolved not to go to her.

Luckily his evenings were taken up with either going to night classes or doing work for them so he told himself he did not have time for the blonde girl or beer. The mornings were such a relief when he could go to the office. Cal had given him a tiny room to himself next door to his own.

Danny loved it. He had never had anything to himself before other than his room at the lodging house, and this was different. Even though it was not completely private because the door between his office and Cal's was always open, he liked it. He liked

231

also that Cal included him in everything. It was not surprising, he thought, that Luke was jealous. Even though he knew that Luke, probably very like his dad, hated the foundry, he also resented that Danny was there, that he was a part of their family in a way.

Danny went with Cal everywhere, soaking up information every second, and when there were meetings with the chemist, with the unions, with the government men, Cal included him. Danny was so proud that he could have burst but never more so than when Cal said to him the week before Christmas, 'Would you like to come to us for Christmas dinner?'

Danny, sitting across the desk from him in Cal's office, was surprised and rather pleased.

'I would rather not, Mr Gray.'

'What else are you going to do?'

Danny didn't answer that.

'Has your mother asked you there?'

'She wouldn't, would she?' Danny said.

The surprising thing was that he was wrong about his mother. She came to the lodging house that very evening. She was so big that Danny doubted the wisdom of her venturing there, but she dismissed his fears

232

with a wave of her hand and said, 'I want you to come home for Christmas.'

'I cannot.' He couldn't call Keir 'my dad' and neither could he call him anything else. 'Mr Gray has asked me to their house.' What else could he tell her? It was the perfect excuse.

'We've never been apart before,' she said.

'I've been stuck here by myself in this room for months,' Danny said. 'What is the difference?'

She couldn't say.

'And I'll bet you have told him you asked me.'

Her face confirmed his suspicions.

'He's not going to want me there. And he still owes me money.' Danny had not meant to mention this.

'For what?'

'For when he got dead drunk. I picked him up off the floor and paid the landlord.'

This was news to his mother, Danny could see. 'I thought he had given it up.'

Danny wanted to laugh. All these years and his mother still believed in fairytales.

'He's trying hard, Danny, he really is.'

'What makes you think I care?' Danny said but he couldn't look at her.

Having turned his mother down Danny felt obliged to go to the Grays' house for Christmas. He even bought a suit from the second-hand shop which fitted him fairly well and some new shoes. He did not know whether he ought to take something with him but since he had nothing he didn't.

'Danny is coming here for his Christmas dinner,' Cal had said to the assembled table the following day when they had tea.

There was silence. His mother sighed.

'I don't understand why he has to come here. Why doesn't he go home?'

'He can't go home,' Cal said, 'and he can't stay by himself on Christmas Day.'

Nobody else said anything.

'He has a horrible room at the boarding house,' Luke said. 'I would hate it.'

'Unfortunately you have no father to quarrel with,' his grandmother said.

Nobody replied. Nobody looked at anybody after that, they all concentrated on what they were eating.

'We shouldn't be celebrating Christmas at all,' she said. 'Not after the year we've had.'

'I don't see that it would help for us to be miserable,' Ailsa said.

'You don't look very miserable to me,

Ailsa,' the older woman said. 'Nobody would think you'd lost your husband.'

'He isn't lost, he's dead,' Margaret said. She had come to hate euphemisms.

'He's lost to me,' her grandmother said so that she regretted her protest. 'My husband and my son within months of one another. A fine Christmas I shall have,' and she got up and left the room.

Ailsa went after her. She had not gone far. It was cold in the hall and dark and she was by the sitting-room fire.

'I'm sorry,' Ailsa said. 'I should have known.' She put her hand over the older woman's hand as it lay on the chair arm and they smiled at each other.

'I think your mother ought to be told about Danny.'

Cal put down the papers as Ailsa closed the door of the study where he was working.

'I did consider it but ... I don't want to spoil her memories of Jaime. Do you think I did the right thing, asking him for Christmas?'

'Yes. It might not be easy but I think it was right.'

Cal smiled at the reassurance.

'The trouble is my mother always thought

I was jealous of Jaime. It's true, of course.'

'I'll tell her,' Ailsa offered.

'I can't let you do that.'

'Why not? I think she would take it better coming from another woman and you've done so much for us. I'll do it.'

She wished she hadn't said so the moment she got out of the room but she knew it was the right thing to do. Why should Cal take the responsibility for something which essentially had nothing to do with him?

She wouldn't do it now, it wasn't fair at this time of night, though his mother slept less and less. How strange that people needed so little sleep when they were old, though it could be because she napped in the afternoons. She would wait until the following day.

The old lady was inclined to disbelieve her, as she would, Ailsa thought, Jaime being her favourite son and it was understandable. She could imagine him as the same little boy Luke had been and it was difficult to get past the child to the man.

To her surprise Mrs Gray sat staring out of the window and said very little. And then Ailsa realized that she did not mind that Jaime had fathered another child. It was not the response Ailsa was looking for and she was taken aback.

Mrs Gray's generation seemed to think, she thought scandalized, that the only things which mattered were whether men were virile and if they could make money. She could recall other old ladies sniggering when boys had got girls 'into trouble' as they called it and the girl was always to blame and always foolish. She tried to put this from her mind. After all, this might work to their advantage.

'Do you know Danny?' she asked.

The old lady looked startled for a moment.

'No, but you have asked him for Christmas Day, haven't you, so I soon shall.'

'We thought you would like to see him because you've lost Jaime and...'

Her tact paid off.

'I would like to meet him. Does he look like Jaime?'

'I think he does but you can judge for yourself.'

'That would be nice. Margaret looks like Callum and poor Luke looks just like you.'

Ailsa enjoyed relating this later to Cal in the privacy of the study when everyone else had gone to bed. I've got my sense of humour back, she thought as she and Cal laughed at his mother's remark.

Jessie had gone back and faced Keir out over the Danny and Christmas issue. He had said nothing, not even when she accused him of getting blind drunk and owing Danny money.

'You have no shame, have you?'

'I didn't remember, that was all.'

'What do you mean?'

'I didn't remember not having paid. I'll go and give him the money.'

'You are so stupid,' she said, close up, her eyes blazing. 'Danny doesn't give a damn about the money, it's you he cares about. Doesn't the fact that you were his dad for so long mean anything to you? He loves you. For the love of God, Keir, go and see him. I won't ever ask…' She clutched at herself in sudden pain and he said,

'Sit yourself down and stop getting worked up.'

'I can't help it. I miss Danny and I'm sorry but…'

'Here.' He drew her over to the nearest chair and helped her into it.

'I have prayed for the baby to be a boy,' she said and that was when Keir was ashamed of himself yet again.

He had, he thought cynically, spent so much of his life feeling apologetic for the awful person he was. He wished he could walk away from the man who drank and was ungenerous but he couldn't.

It was who he was. He would have given a lot to be somebody else, to not be the man who couldn't forgive her, who couldn't love Danny any more. That was the trouble, he couldn't love the boy who wasn't his son.

In the end he went to the boarding house and had Danny come to the door of the room and let him in. It was a big room, nice, but he couldn't say so.

He wished for the thousandth time that everything was different, that Danny was his son, and now that they were face to face he found that he had been wrong, he loved Danny. He would always love him and that was the hardest thing of all. He wanted Danny to be his son and it would never happen.

'Your mam wants you to come home for Christmas Day.'

'Mr Gray has asked me there.'

'She said. Danny…'

'You couldn't say you wanted me to, could you?' Danny said bitterly. 'Anyhow, I've said I will go to the Grays.'

'Maybe that's where you should be,' Keir said.

'Oh aye, it's right where I should be,' Danny said.

'You could come to tea with us.'

'I don't want to come to tea with you.'

'I can't go back and tell your mam that.'

'Go back and tell her anything you like,' Danny said.

Keir dreaded going home, he dreaded that Jessie would be waiting for him and so she was, standing alone there, tired and white-faced and huge with the baby and all she said to him was, 'Well?'

'He wouldn't.'

She let go of her breath, held her back and turned away, almost in tears, he knew.

'I'm sorry, Jessie, I did try.'

'Aye, well, never mind. There's not much we can do,' and they didn't talk about it any more.

It was the middle of the night when Jessie's waters broke and right from the beginning Keir knew that something was wrong. She woke him when it happened, clutched at his hand and she was sweating so much that her skin was slick.

'I'll go for the doctor,' he offered.

She begged him not to leave her.

'Our Shannon will go.'

'I'm not having her on the streets at this time of night. It's not safe.'

He put on his clothes and left her even though she tried not to let go of him and went as quietly as he could into the other bedroom. He did not want to wake up the bairns.

Shannon came to abruptly as he shook her.

'Sh,' he cautioned, whispering. 'Get dressed. Your mam's bad. I'll have to go for Dr Philips.'

'I can go.'

'No, you stay here with her. I won't be long.'

When he opened the outside door it was snowing big thick flakes. He turned up the collar of his jacket and ran down the bank towards the town.

It was a long wait. Jessie was soon in pain and Shannon felt sure that nothing should have started yet. She breathed very carefully and Shannon tried to think reassuring thoughts. Her mother had already had five children. Why should this one be any different?

The children slept on, there was nothing but her, her mam and this room with its one dim light, and beyond it the empty street when she occasionally pulled at the curtains in hope that her dad was on his way back with the doctor. From there you could see the beck and the houses on the other side of the cliff but the narrow steep cobbled road was empty for so long that she despaired.

Keir banged and banged on the door of the doctor's house which was opposite the foundry. Eventually a woman came to the door. She said that the doctor was already out, he wouldn't be long and closed the door.

He stood for what felt like for ever, getting colder and colder and more and more worried. Then his heart lifted as he saw a man in a long overcoat and a black bag. Keir explained briefly. The doctor nodded and went with him.

Shannon was so relieved when she heard them come in that she was almost happy. Unfortunately the noise woke one of the children, who woke the other two. When her father and the doctor tramped upstairs she went back into the other bedroom and tried to reassure them, lying down with them until they went back to sleep.

Then she made her way downstairs and raked over the warm ashes and started the fire up. She sat there over it while the snow went on falling, waiting for the light which she thought would never come.

Upstairs Keir hovered while the doctor examined Jessie. Then the doctor came over, saying in a low voice, 'We must get your wife to hospital. Where is the nearest telephone?'

'I don't know.'

'Then you must go back to my house and tell my wife to telephone for us. I shall stay here until the ambulance arrives.'

Jessie had never felt like this before in her life, the pain and the heat, neither of which would go away. This could not be happening to her body. All her children's births had caused her pain but there had not been anything like this. She began to find it all very confusing. There were voices which she ceased to recognize and she did not know where she was.

She wanted to go home. She wanted Keir to take her home, back to the little house on the hill, back to her bairns, but she reached the point where she would have settled for being anywhere that was not here, in all this pain, in all this burning heat. Where was she?

She called and called for him but he did not come.

It was lonely here. She wished and wished that he would come for her. The pain and heat were getting worse and worse until she did not think that she could bear it. She tried to speak but no words came out, nothing happened. It was getting dark and the space in which she existed was somehow all inside herself.

It was strange but everything which was not inside her body ceased to hold importance. Everything was concentrated on her, on a smaller and smaller space all the time.

At long last the pain and the burning began to ebb away and she was so pleased, so relieved. Soon he would come for her and everything would be all right.

She felt as though she was curled up like a child, like a baby in a womb, curled up there and safe where there was no pain and no burning heat, safe inside the space there, clear of everything and it was growing light at last. The light was golden, all-encompassing, gentle.

In the end it was easier for Shannon to take the children downstairs because they kept waking up at different times. Once Keir had put his head round the bedroom door and said, 'I'm going to go and ring for an ambulance,' there was no peace, nor did she expect any.

She would have liked to be able to clear her mind, to take her rosary and run to the church and pray to the Blessed Virgin for her mother's life, but she couldn't. She had to content herself with praying silently and try to keep the children busy.

The two older ones knew that it was almost Christmas morning and knew also that they would have a present each.

In the end she gave them their stockings, took them into the front room and lit the fire there. She wanted to get them as far away as she could from what was happening upstairs and they spent time reaching for oranges, nuts, a chocolate bar each which they promptly ate and a tiny game for them which she and her mam had bought at the store earlier that week. Shannon could not bear to think about it.

The little games had tiny silver baubles inside which had to be placed on indentations and then they formed a face or a scene, could be shaken and started again. It kept them busy.

It was almost daybreak by the time her dad came back. She heard the ambulance arrive in the lane to the side of the house and some commotion. The stair rods clinked as somebody went up and then she heard her dad cry out and the sound of the doctor's low voice. She was desperate to go to him but she could not leave the little ones alone by the fire.

More footsteps coming down after a while, the stair rods banging back into place even more heavily, the door clashed, the ambulance drew away. The house was silent.

Shannon didn't understand. Had they both gone with her mother? Surely her dad would have come and told her if he was going to the hospital. He wouldn't just have left. And then she heard movement above.

She put the fireguard up against the blaze, told Veronica to watch the other two and then she closed the door behind her so that neither of the little ones would come running after her. She crept through the cold kitchen, where the neglected fire was black cinders, and made her way as softly as she could up the stairs and on to the landing.

She opened the door. The fire had gone

out though the room still kept most of its heat. The lamp burned and she could see her father sitting on the bed and her mother lying there. As Shannon entered the room the baby began to cry and then to scream. Nobody moved.

'Dad?'

He turned and she saw his expression, disbelief and something more.

'She's dead,' he said.

Shannon stared at her mother, thinking she had not heard properly, while the baby screamed even more loudly from the cot which up till now had been their Theresa's. She wanted to run out. She wanted to make the children the excuse and run downstairs. She wished she had not come up here. Everything would still be all right if she had not come up here.

He was making some kind of dreadful joke. Her mother had always been fine when she gave birth. Once she had had the baby before anyone could reach her. Had it been Theresa or Mary? She couldn't remember now.

She stared, waiting for her mother to call her name, and when nothing happened she went over and lifted the baby from the cot. It had nothing on it but a blanket and from there she could see the mess the bed was in and how still her mother was.

'Dad?'

This time he didn't respond.

'Dad?'

Slowly he turned and looked at her.

'Take the baby downstairs and see to the bairns,' she said.

'You take him.'

It was a him? Shannon tried to concentrate. 'I have to sort this out.'

'No,' he said.

'All right, go and get Mrs Leary.'

He didn't respond.

'Dad–'

'I heard you. Take the baby and go downstairs.'

'But–'

'Go.'

She went. She heated some boiled water in a pan on the sitting-room fire and gave it to the baby in a bottle. He was thirsty. He drank and then he stopped crying.

She gave him a wash in warm water and put him into the smallest nightie she could find in the chest of drawers. She put a little cap on his head and booties on his feet and then she put him into the pram which was very old but had been used for them all. She wrapped him up neatly and firmly and she rocked the pram by its handle and he was soon asleep.

Mary wanted her mother.

'She's tired. She's just had a baby. She's gone to sleep,' Shannon said. 'You'll see her later. Now I'm going to take you to bed.'

They didn't resist. Full of chocolate, orange and nuts, they were tired and the excitement of Christmas was already over for them. She tucked them into bed and when she was satisfied that they slept she went back downstairs.

She could have taken the baby into bed with her but she didn't want to go back upstairs again so she lay down on the settle and closed her eyes. She didn't sleep. Her body had gone into shock. She lay there and listened and in the silence she heard her father begin to cry from above.

It was like no other Christmas Day had ever been, the snow like a shroud for her mother. She went around early to the house three doors up and Mrs Leary clicked her tongue over Shannon's mam dying at what was meant to be such a joyous time.

'I don't like to ask, it being Christmas, but–'

'Oh, don't think anything of it, honey-lamb.' Mrs Leary called everybody 'honey-lamb'. 'Come away in here a minute and then we'll go round and sort everything out.'

Keir was downstairs when they got back, Shannon was glad of that. Then she and Mrs Leary took hot water and soap and towels and they washed her mother's body. Shannon, who had never seen her mother naked before, was astonished at how right it felt to perform this service for someone you loved who had died.

Mrs Leary kept up a stream of talk and Shannon knew that she didn't have to reply, it was a form of comfort, it split the silence. They put her mother into white and Mrs Leary took the bed linen and said she would do some washing in the morning if it promised to be a fine day and Shannon was not to worry about anything.

Once it was done and Mrs Leary had gone Shannon gave the children their breakfast. Her father sat at the table, silent, eating nothing, staring out of the window at the snow in the back yard. When they were finished eating the children clamoured to see their mother.

'You're going to have to tell them,' Shannon said, close to his ear.

So he did. He told them that their mother had gone to heaven. No purgatory for Jessie, then, she thought, dazed, but then what else could you tell children? They didn't understand of course but then who did?

Shannon distracted them as best she could with games and gave them the Christmas dinner such as it was, rabbit stew and apple tart. Her father ate nothing and neither did she. When the meal was over and they were beginning to ask once again when their mother would come back, and the baby had accepted a bottle and gone to sleep and she had cleared up, she said to him, 'Our Danny has to know. Do you want me to tell him?'

Danny spent most of Christmas morning remembering the past Christmases at home, remembering them probably a lot better than they really had been, he thought. What did they call it – rose-coloured spectacles? But even though he tried he could not stop thinking of how happy he had been at the little house up the bank with his mam and dad and the girls.

He missed Shannon and he felt guilty thinking of how his mam had toiled her way to his lodging and tried to get him to go back home. He missed his dad, not the person he was but the way that they had been.

He thought of the bairns opening their stockings and their delight at the small treasures, and most difficult of all somehow was the fact that he could have afforded to buy presents for them all this year better than anything they had ever seen before but he hadn't.

He was nervous going to the big house officially for the first time. He felt so out of place and although they were kind he could hardly eat anything.

Phoebe was not really surprised to find Cal at her door in the middle of Christmas morning. He kissed her in the gloom of the hall, just on the cheek, and proffered a small box.

'Your Christmas present,' he said.

Phoebe did not know what to say and stuttered her thanks, not taking him into the sitting room but the small morning room which looked out over the back of the property. There she tore the paper off and flipped up the lid and it was a ring, tiny seed pearls with an oval-shaped ruby in the middle. She felt her cheeks warm.

'I know it's overdue,' he said. 'I think it won't be long until this war is over and it is almost a year since Jaime died so…'

'It's exquisite,' Phoebe said and in a feeling of gratitude she went over and kissed him. Cal got hold of her and kissed her on the mouth in a lingering way that she could not help but like.

'Perhaps we should set a wedding date. Even your father can hardly object.'

There was therefore no reason for Phoebe to panic. She felt like a little girl being given the wrong Christmas box, she could not brush away the feelings and she could not pretend to herself that her parents were not very pleased, their faces gave them away. They urged Cal to stay and have a drink, her father found champagne which he said he had long been saving for such an occasion. Cal did not stay long. Her mother had put out hot food on the dining-room table and people were already crowding into the hall.

'I'll see you later,' he said before he left. Phoebe watched him as he walked down the drive. She turned the ring over on her finger. It felt strange there, too beautiful for her worn workaday hands.

Fifteen

Christmas Day had dawned cold, wet, most of the snow already melted, showing the green of the lawns. This was not how Christmas was meant to be, Margaret thought, but then was Christmas ever how it was meant to be?

They were at war, still. She was beginning to think that it would never end, not before it had taken everybody and everything. People were exhausted. Cal kept falling asleep in the evenings before the study fire and he was quiet to the point where it was difficult being in a room with him. She had ventured to ask, one evening that week, when she went to wake him up to eat dinner, 'Do you think we're winning?'

'We'll come through,' was all he said.

She wasn't sure she believed him but at night when she awoke she tried to hear the reassuring words while she worried about it.

Ailsa was not surprised when Christmas Day turned out to be quite different than she had expected. Danny appeared at the front door at eleven and the moment he stepped inside the house it was as though a transformation had taken place. He was dressed up. Ailsa had never seen him that way before and he was to her eyes exactly as Jaime had been when she had fallen in love with him when they were young.

The illusion didn't last. Danny had not Jaime's gracefulness nor his elegance of speech. Jaime had had a soft cultured voice whereas Danny had a thick local accent. He was also a much more brisk, practical person. In fact, though she would not have said so to him, Danny was like Cal, could have been his son.

It was obvious from the beginning however that the old lady saw nothing but the return of her dead child. She didn't say much but her face shone and she spent the entire Christmas meal looking across the table at him. Danny seemed not to notice.

The meal was the best that could be contrived, two of their own chickens which had been stewed because they were old, sprouts and potatoes from the garden and then a good fire to sit over as the day drew in.

The children went off to the beach, Cal's mother retreated to bed during the dark afternoon and Ailsa felt strangely bereft.

They spent a long time on the beach while the day greyed itself towards evening. Danny half expected Shannon to appear. She must know he was there and he was irritated and resentful that she did not turn up. He would have felt much better if he could have seen her that day.

When they got back to the house it was dark. Mr Gray came into the hall.

'Mr Logan is here to see you, Danny,' he said, 'in the study.'

The study was Danny's least favourite room in the house, it reminded him of his lack of education. The books were blue, red, green, black and most of them had gold lettering, and some which he assumed were valuable were behind glass.

He wasn't really very surprised to see Keir standing on the hearthrug, no doubt Jessie had sent him there to see if he could persuade Danny to go to them. Though part of him wanted so much to be with them his hurt pride would not allow him to be glad.

He didn't look at the tall slender man he had loved so much. How could he have loved such a drunken failure? Keir didn't even have a decent suit, yet he still managed to give off the air of an Irish vagabond, stupidly wild and gallant looking, like somebody out of one of those bloody daft poems you learned off by heart at school.

How did he do that, Danny wondered, after the life he had led? The dark eyes, the unruly black hair and the pale flawless skin made him look not much more than a child. It was difficult not to love him. Danny's heart ached. The eyes were as impenetrable as always.

'I'm not coming to the house.'

'Danny–'

'I'm not. I don't know how you thought you could persuade me when my mam tried just the other day.'

'Danny–'

'Mr Gray asked me to come here and I belong here. I feel right like I never did with you. I knew all along you couldn't be my dad. Nobody as … as stupid and feckless as you could ever have been my dad.' Danny almost added 'so there' but he didn't because it sounded childish even before he said it.

Unable to stand the way Keir was not taking up the words being scattered around him like bullets, Danny became silent. It was only then that he realized something was wrong.

Keir wasn't looking at him. Was it shame

that he could not persuade Danny to go to the house on so important a day, did he not want to tell his wife he had failed yet again and at something else?

'Your mother, she...'

'She had the baby?' Danny said helpfully.

'Yes.'

'And was it a boy?'

'Aye, it was—'

'How grand for you. A son of your own at last. You must be so pleased. As though you had nowt of your own to start with.' Danny was shouting, even he could hear it. He thought the study rang with his words, that somehow they went through the books or bounced off them, echoing.

'Have you called him Danny to replace me?'

Now Keir looked shocked. He said nothing.

'What have you called him then, Jesus?' Danny started to laugh. 'It's right, don't you think, being born at Christmas?'

Keir didn't reply and Danny wasn't feeling very good by this time but he could not help going on with the idea.

'Jesus Logan. It has a grand sound. What are you going to call him, then?'

Keir still didn't reply. Danny made himself

wait and wait this time, until the silence was knee deep and the man on the hearthrug had given up his half-hearted attempt at speech and was concentrating on the fire.

He was not quite turned away and Danny had cause to wish that he had been, because as the Christmas afternoon gave itself up to evening a single small tear slid slowly down Keir's pale cheek. That was when he turned away.

Danny stared and then his heart misgave him.

'Dad?'

Keir shook his head as though that would take care of the tear.

'She's dead,' he said.

'What?'

'My Jessie. She's dead.'

'But she can't be.'

'In the night. She died from having the baby.'

Danny stared at him, went on and on until time ceased to matter, staring at him, thinking somehow that Keir might be telling lies because it could not be the truth.

'But she's … she's had lots of children.'

'This was one too many,' Keir said. 'I'm sorry, Danny.' And he walked past Danny and out of the door.

Sixteen

Phoebe opened the back door with some distrust. The day had turned dark or had never got light somehow. She thought it had taken her some time to understand that somebody was demanding entrance, though who it could be on a cold wet Christmas night she could not think.

She was exhausted. The last of the revellers had finally gone and she and her parents, having cleared everything away, were looking forward to a quiet evening by the fire.

She did think that it might be Cal. She unbolted the door at top and bottom and turned the huge key and there stood Shannon, a picture of misery. Phoebe felt the sympathy issue from her lips in a little, 'Oh,' before she took Shannon's sleeve and urged her inside.

'I don't mean to get in the road, miss, I know it's Christmas Day.'

Phoebe hushed her, took her into the drawing room where her parents were sitting over the fire with a cup of tea. A big fire blazed in there, Phoebe had a stack of dry logs for such occasions. Shannon attempted to hover in the doorway but Mrs Wilson got up in concern and came to her.

'Why, you're wet through,' she said, 'here, take off your coat.'

Shannon did so. Phoebe wanted to urge her to say whatever she had come to say and distracted herself by offering tea. It was only when Shannon had refused that she launched into an obviously prepared speech.

'I only came to tell you that I won't be able to come any more. My mam died this morning and…' Whatever was meant to come after the 'and' never arrived. Shannon choked and began to cry.

'Oh, my dear,' Mrs Wilson said and sat her down, and that was when Mr Wilson poured sherry and insisted on her drinking it. Shannon took the glass, wobbled it to her lips and drank. Phoebe was unable to get anything coherent out of Shannon and despite her protests insisted on going back with her. It had stopped raining by then. Her father had said as she left, 'I'll come to the bottom of the bank for you in an hour.'

She nodded and followed Shannon out of the door.

Phoebe had been in a good many poor places in her life so she did know what to expect. And she knew that Shannon's father was a hopeless drunk and also that he was a dreadful man, famous for fighting and without a vestige of respectability, so she was not prepared for the sight that met her eyes when she stepped down into the kitchen of Number 3, Lane End.

She had met many uneducated, ignorant louts in her time and thought herself equal to them. Would he shout that she had come into his home? Would the children be running about screaming, dirty and half-naked? Would there be empty beer bottles under the table and the place in grubby disarray?

The fire was bright, the black surround shone and in its reflection two children were asleep on the settle, one with a thumb in her mouth. There was a thick blanket over them for warmth. In a pram further across a baby slept and sitting on the kitchen stool by the fire was the tall figure of a man not much older than herself, with a small child in his arms.

To Phoebe's consternation she could not help but stare. He was in his shirtsleeves as though he had spent a great deal of time getting the children to sleep. He had pale skin and dark eyes and thick black hair and a slender grief-stricken face, the lines cut into it with lack of sleep and concern.

'No, please don't get up,' Phoebe said. 'I'm Phoebe Wilson. I only came to see if I could help.'

Phoebe had never in a man's presence felt anything but plain, skinny and stupid but Keir Logan's gaze had the same effect as a deep warm bath and his voice was pure music.

'Why, it was good of you, Miss Wilson,' he said, 'but as you can see we are managing.'

'You are indeed,' Phoebe said, not knowing where to look. And then she was horrified at herself. This man's wife was lying dead upstairs and she … she could not help seeing him as a man.

He was tall when he got to his feet and totally focused on what he was doing so if he did drink it seemed to Phoebe that he had not done so in many days. She was half-inclined to excuse herself and leave but she couldn't walk back through the town by herself and besides it would seem rude.

'What can I do to help?' she offered.

'Give us your company,' he said. Shannon made the tea, and the child slept in his arms. Phoebe drank her tea and wondered who this woman was who had never loved before now.

No wonder she had not really wanted to marry Cal and how dreadful that she should have such overwhelming feelings so indiscriminately. She should somehow have been able to control and disperse them but she could not.

When she had drunk her tea however she felt that she must go. He gave the child to Shannon and insisted on walking her home. Phoebe was very sorry for Jessie Logan but she could not help being glad of his company.

The night had cleared and all the stars were out. All the drunks were out too but nobody approached her, spoke or even shouted across the street. Mr Logan made no conversation and it was only when they reached the vicarage gates that Phoebe managed, 'I'm so very sorry about your wife.'

All he said was, 'Thank you. She was my lass, my only one.'

Phoebe thought for a moment. Then she was about to say goodnight when he said, 'I always meant to say that it was good of you to give our Shannon a job. She won't be able to come any more now.'

'But she...' Phoebe said and then stopped. She had not thought until then how Shannon's life would change, she had been too shocked to absorb the information earlier so she uttered a goodnight and trudged up the drive towards her home and he stood, watching, until she reached the door.

She was in the hall when her father heard her.

'I was just going to come for you. You haven't walked back alone?'

'No, Mr Logan walked me,' she said.

Her father looked at her.

'And what is he like?'

'He's ... in a very bad way about his wife,' Phoebe said.

'But he cared sufficiently about your safety to see you back. That was fine. Do come and sit by the fire with us.'

Phoebe could not put from her mind the vision of Keir Logan with a small child sleeping in his arms. How old was he? He had five children. He could not have been more than thirty-four or five, the same age as she was. However would he manage now?

She didn't sleep. All night her mind presented her with every word that he had said, with his lovely lilting voice, his dark shocked eyes, the clean poor little house.

266

She resolved a dozen times that night not to think about him any more and a dozen times her mind slid back to him without any care for anything else.

She tried to think about Cal. After all he had presented her with an engagement ring that day, a valuable beautiful ring as token of his intent to marry her.

She thought of tears in her mother's eyes and she knew what they had thought, that the war was almost over, that it was time to move on, that they would have the joy of a wedding and the possibility of grand-children, that she, for all she was an old maid, was engaged to the most influential man in the area.

She thought about how Cal had kissed her and wished he had done it again. Somehow it was as though the relationship was barely sealed, in spite of the ring and the kiss, as though Cal was reluctant.

He didn't seem reluctant. A reluctant man would hardly have come over on Christmas morning bearing a ruby for the girl he said he loved and wanted to marry, yet there was something held back. She did not know what it was but she worried about Ailsa and Cal together in the house. Ailsa had nobody now and Cal had always liked her.

Danny stood in the centre of the room after Keir had gone until he heard a noise, and there was Margaret standing in the doorway as though unsure whether to come in.

'Has he gone?'

'Yes.'

'Are you going over to see your mother?'

Danny tried to look at the floor because he thought it might save him. He went on looking at the floor, wishing she would go out and leave him alone, but she came in.

'You should go over and see her, you know, it isn't right.'

Still Danny could say nothing.

'Has she had the baby? Is that what he came here for?'

'I have to go. Tell Mr Gray I'm sorry.'

'Go? Go where?'

'I have to.'

Danny tried to get out of the house but he was not seeing anything by then and couldn't find the door.

'What is it? What's the matter?'

Danny wrenched open the front door, ran up the garden, around the side of the house and out into the lane. And Margaret, damn her, he thought, ran after him.

'Danny?'

'Go away!' was all he could manage. He ran much faster, he ran and ran until he was clear of the cold wet village and until she had ceased to run after him, so he thought, and then he had the beach to himself, there was not a soul on it and he was glad of that because he couldn't run any more. His knees buckled under him and he gave himself up to the misery, put his hands over his face.

'Danny?'

She was still there.

'Why don't you just go away, for God's sake?' he shouted.

'Oh, whatever's the matter?' She got down beside him and they were low on the beach, the tide had just gone down and the sand was wet, sucking you in. Danny wished it would suck him in and drown him.

'My mam's dead. I didn't go and see her and now I never can. I didn't go because I wanted her to feel bad about what she did and I wanted him to feel bad and he should, he should, but now…'

Margaret sat there not saying anything for a long time and he didn't say anything either. There was no sound but the washing of the waves across the beach.

It was quite dark by this time and as it

grew colder and colder, so Danny thought he would not want to move for the rest of his life.

She got close and began to talk to him, not anything startling, not anything helpful or about his mam or how he shouldn't feel bad, but just about the way that the tide was coming up the beach and how if he didn't move soon they would be wet through.

He couldn't bring himself to do anything but he could feel the cold water washing around him, the soft, wet sand and the way that the tide got into everything. His feet were soon saturated. Although he should have told her to go and leave him there, he didn't so that she was soon soaked too, the bottom third of her coat was in water.

It was not until there was six inches of water around him that Danny moved. The tide had a long way to come in yet, the wind was bitter on his face and his feet were so cold by now that when he did try to move it was difficult, both because they were numb and because the water had washed them into the wet sand and it felt solid.

They walked back to the Grays' house as quickly as their wet clothes and shoes allowed them. Mr Gray came out of the sitting room as soon as they got in as though he had been worried. By his face he had been.

'Are you all right?' he said.

Margaret was not, Danny thought, the sort of person to beat about the bush.

'Danny's mother died having the baby,' she said. He was glad she said it because he was beginning to think he would never speak again and never want anything again and never be warm and dry again. Then Mrs Gray came into the hall and Mr Gray told her immediately. She was practical like women were, like his mam had always been.

She brought towels and told them to take off their shoes and she sat them by the fire, not in the sitting room for fear, Danny thought, that too many people might upset him. If he wanted to be upset maybe it would be better to do it in private, so they sat by the study fire. But he didn't really want to be there either because he could not wipe from his mind the vision of Keir almost turned away and crying.

Mr Gray brought them tea with brandy and Danny sat, sipping his drink, wrapped in an enormous soft rug. When he felt better Mrs Gray escorted him upstairs into a big bedroom where a fire blazed, showed him where the bathroom was, the pyjamas on the bed. After he thanked her and she had gone Danny washed and undressed and got into bed and it was warm and the fire was crackling, he could see it.

It was, he thought, exactly the right thing because he was worn out. He felt protected, looked after, just as he had felt in the old days when he had lived with his mam and dad.

Now he had nobody, Keir didn't want him and his mam was dead, but he was here in the house where his real dad had grown up. That was a strange and for the first time ever a comforting feeling. Maybe in spite of the fact that his mam was dead, he had finally come home. It was his last thought before he fell asleep.

Seventeen

It was the middle of March. It seemed to Keir as though the winter had gone on for ever. He had buried his wife and since then he had gone to work most days and Shannon had looked after the children. But life had slowed and he was beginning to think that he would never be able to think of anything but Jessie's death and the awful way that he had treated her after he found out that Danny was not his.

It was mid-evening. He had not gone back to the pub. He could not afford to do so and he didn't have the heart. He had to face his friends at work and their sympathetic faces, he couldn't do it in the evenings. Now that there was no Jessie to come home to he didn't want to go out. No Jessie and no Danny. It was like a never-ending nightmare.

He heard the banging on the door and, leaving Shannon with the children, he got up to open it. It was only then that he recognized the woman from the vicarage. He felt sorry for her, she was so skinny, so plain. She was an old maid. But then of course she would be. She was engaged to marry his employer. What on earth was she doing there on this bitterly cold night?

The road beyond his house was glittering with frost and he could hear the waves crashing up the beach.

'I want to talk to you, Mr Logan,' she said.

'You'd better come in, then.'

'No, thank you, you come out.'

Keir was in his shirtsleeves but it was obvious she wanted to say something to him that she didn't want Shannon to hear. He was right. He stepped outside into the bitter air and looked past her until she said, 'It's about Shannon.'

'What about her?'

'She wants to be a nun.'

'I know that. There's nothing I can do. I have four small children, Miss Wilson. What do you suggest I do with them?'

'That's not Shannon's problem. You can't expect her to give up her life for your children. Can't you see how worn out she is, how thin?'

'You have a solution to the problem, do you?'

'You could employ somebody.'

'Now you're being funny,' he said.

She was actually blushing, he could see in the moonlight the way that her face changed, darkened and how she shifted her feet. He didn't understand why she was so discomforted.

She didn't say anything else and the cold was getting through his thin clothes.

'I should go in. I have to be up early. I'm a furnaceman.'

She had nothing more to say, it seemed. She turned away. He wanted to say something, anything, because she had been so kind and there was no reason why she should be. She cared about Shannon, that much was obvious.

'Thank you, Miss Wilson.'

She turned back.

'For thinking about our Shannon. I do care, I just don't see what I can do about it. It was good of you. Why don't you come in and see her, just for a moment or two?'

She let herself be persuaded and went inside. The children loved visitors and clustered around her knees when she sat down. Shannon gave her the baby and she seemed to like holding it.

'We've called him Michael,' Shannon said and she said it was a lovely name. Keir thought she would have said that to any name at all.

She seemed reluctant to leave but didn't say much either. Finally she gave the baby back to Shannon and said she must go.

Keir followed her out. She smiled slightly in the moonlight and then he remembered his manners like he hadn't remembered them in days. He said, 'Hang on a minute,' and he went back inside and took his jacket off the nail behind the door, and as Shannon looked up from where she was feeding the baby by the fire, he said, 'I'm going out for a few minutes.'

Shannon's expression darkened.

'I'm not going to the pub. I'm just going to see Miss Wilson back across the street. All right?'

He put his jacket on without a word and went back outside.

It was the second time he had seen Phoebe to the vicarage gates. She protested but he knew he was right.

'You shouldn't have come,' he said. 'I'll see you back.'

'I don't need seeing back,' she said.

Neither seemed to know what to say after that but Keir felt obliged to make what small talk he could. He wasn't used to women except Jessie, and Miss Wilson talked posh and lived in a great big house and had had servants before the war. Her dad had made a lot of money doing something, Keir couldn't remember what.

'So you're getting married,' he said and then hoped it didn't sound interfering and abrupt.

'It would seem so.'

'Aye, well. That'll be nice.'

'The war won't last much longer, they say. We could be married in the summer, I suppose, or ... in the autumn.'

'Have you been waiting a long time?'

'No, it's just ... my brothers were both killed. They were fliers.'

'Aye, I know. Brave lads.'

'Yes, and ... my parents would dearly like grandchildren.'

'I'm sure they would. Well, it's very nearly spring so you probably won't have to wait much longer.'

There were drunks fighting in the street, servicemen, he thought, they had some kind of uniform on. Sometimes they were funny about men who weren't in uniform though Keir knew as well as anybody that specialist jobs like his were just as important. He manoeuvred Miss Wilson around them by holding her arm for a few moments until she got the idea.

'I see what you mean,' she said in half apology when they were safely past. 'They weren't here before.'

It was a long dark lane up to the vicarage and he was inclined to tell her that if she had been his daughter he wouldn't have been very happy for her to walk down there on her own either. Then he remembered that she was much older than Shannon but he still wanted to tell her.

'I don't like to leave my parents.'

He thought she meant she didn't like to go out in the dark and leave them. She saw his confused face and she said, 'By getting married.'

'But Mr Gray's house is only across town.'

'I know and I know they are glad for me but…'

'You see, I think our Shannon feels like that about me.'

That made her smile for some reason.

'My parents are old, Mr Logan. You aren't old.'

'I feel old.'

'If I could … find you somebody to look after the children would you let Shannon do as she wanted?'

'I can't afford anybody,' he said.

'But would you?'

'No.'

'You don't want anybody in your house?'

Keir tried to ignore the impatience he felt.

'It isn't that but somebody would have to pay. Later, when the children are older–'

'That will take years. That will take Shannon's young life. Don't you understand?'

'I do, yes.'

They had reached the end of the lane. Further on there was the new vicarage and then the church with its tall spire and beyond that was the country. He opened the gates and walked her up the drive and she said, 'You don't need to take me any further. Good night, Mr Logan,' so that Keir thought he had unwittingly offended her.

He waited until she slammed the door and then he went the short way home, but cutting out the street where his favourite pub lay.

As Phoebe closed the door she met her mother's surprised gaze.

'I didn't know you'd gone out. Is it safe?'

'I only went for a walk for a few minutes,' Phoebe lied. She wondered who this dreadful new person was who was in thrall to a common man whose wife had just died and would do anything for a few moments of his company.

She shed her hat, coat, gloves and scarf and followed her mother into the drawing room, to find that her mother had been upstairs and unearthed her old wedding dress.

'We can't consider this yet, there's still a war on.'

'It will be over soon,' her mother said, 'and we will deserve a beautiful wedding and you have waited so long for it, my darling, that we will spare no expense. I want the whole district here. I'm going to have my day with those women who have looked pityingly at me when talking about their married daughters and their grandchildren.'

That made Phoebe laugh. 'Mother!'

'You're marrying the most eligible man in the area and I want everybody to know it.'

Phoebe wanted to run out of the room, preferably out of the house. Perhaps, she thought, I'm losing my mind. All she could think about was the way that Keir stood in the dark doorway of his tiny house and invited her in. What would he think if he knew that she wanted to be in his presence more than she had ever wanted anything in her life? How awful.

Eighteen

Hitler was dead. Cal stood, staring at the wireless, and it was strange but among the feelings of relief was a strange reluctance to go forward. It was May, it was spring. The people were rejoicing in the streets. Cal didn't feel like rejoicing. He felt as though in some ways for many people the war would never be over. For those like Phoebe's parents, who had lost both their sons, the repercussions would go on and on.

When he went to the vicarage he sensed a desperation on them, a brightness which he knew he alone could ease.

Phoebe, in spite of his promises, looked to him as though she would dwindle into pale greyness, as if she might disappear altogether if they did not marry.

He had finally pinned her to a date. They were to be married this Saturday. Her father and mother had told him that they were delighted. Phoebe, he sensed, was not. He had tried to talk to her about it and she had talked vaguely of shortages and having no suitable dress and not looked at him until he had said to her one cool, rainy evening by the library fire in her house, earlier that week, 'If you don't want to do this you only have to say.'

He could not think why she would not want to marry him, having gone this far. Surely she knew her own mind to the extent that she would have told him sooner if she had decided differently. He did not consider himself a vain man but he was well off and Phoebe, as far as he was aware, had had no other offers.

It had occurred to him that if she did not marry soon she might be too old to have children and everybody would be disappointed. He was not that bothered when he thought honestly about it. It surprised him. Often now he would go into Danny's office and Danny would look up and Cal could see his own reflection in the boy.

It was strange to Cal that out of Jessie and Jaime's youthful mistake he should have gained so much. In a way, Keir Logan had gifted Danny to him. How could any man give up such a prize for any reason? He was fond, of course, of Margaret and Luke but he had not for them the gut-wrenching love that he felt for the boy who had become part of their household.

Danny loved him. Cal knew he did. They spent their days together at work and Cal had never cared as much for the place as he did now, seeing it through Danny's eyes, and Danny was changing. His use of language was more sophisticated, his manners and bearing were good. Keir and Jessie, Cal thought, had somehow made Danny into the man he would become and industry and prosperity would do the rest.

Danny would have the foundry one day completely for his and Cal was glad of it. Luke was not the man to run it. In fact the twins had not a useful bone in their bodies. Sometimes he despaired and then he thought of Danny and was glad. Danny was his son.

Phoebe, startled by the remark, had gazed across the library fire at him and said, 'Whatever do you mean?'

Cal didn't want to go on but felt obliged. 'You lack enthusiasm,' he said.

'It isn't that.'

'What is it, then?'

'It's just – just weddings. They're so very difficult,' she said. She smiled and added, 'This is my first, have patience with me,' and then changed the subject.

Saturday was a warmer day than many had been of late. Phoebe had barely slept and was pleased when the dawn finally broke red beyond the houses. She lay in bed feeling like crying and being stern with herself. As the shadows left the room she could see the white dress hanging on the outside of the wardrobe. It had been her mother's, altered slightly, her mother tut-tutting with a mouthful of pins at how thin she had become.

It didn't suit her, Phoebe had thought, when she had tried it on the day before and her mother had told her untruthfully that she looked beautiful in it.

She had watched her mother in the mirror and tried to smile because she knew that she had to go through with this, it was her parents' only chance of grandchildren and her sole opportunity to marry. The feelings of sickness and panic would die when Cal put the ring on her finger. Everything would be all right.

The church was for the first time too close to the house. The vicarage looked as it had always looked, as though it was built to go with the church, whereas the new vicarage was a square brick house, built just before the war. It had no sweeping staircase, no huge kitchen with an Aga, no outbuildings, no orchard, no view across the valley.

This house which she had always loved so much as a haven would be her home no more after today. She would have to go and live with Cal, sleep in his bed, put up with his mother and worst of all with Ailsa, who looked younger now than she had done when she arrived. Ailsa, Phoebe thought, was beautiful and she lived in Cal's house as though she were the mistress of it. How on earth would they put up with one another?

Phoebe could not eat the breakfast which her mother brought for her in bed. After that she had to get up and bathe and wash her hair and put up with the chatter of the hairdresser and submit to her mother's idea of make-up.

Shannon and Margaret were to be her bridesmaids and they seemed excited and happy. She had nobody to talk to, no one to confide in.

When she was dressed she looked in the mirror and thought that what colour there had been in the make-up drained away because of the white dress.

They walked to church, it being such a little way, her mother went ahead and then she on her father's arm. The walk went too quickly. She did not recollect what he said to her though he talked all the way there. He was smiling when they got to the gloom of the church porch and Phoebe stumbled, stopped.

The organist had struck up the music, Shannon and Margaret, in pretty blue dresses, were standing, waiting to follow her down the aisle. She could see the guests, a lot of people from the village had come to see her married. She thought Cal had invited the whole workforce and their families. It was not a small occasion, the church was full and as her eyes searched pew after pew it was only then that she realized who she was looking for. And he was not there.

Keir Logan would be at home minding his children, he would not be able to see Shannon, though being Catholics perhaps they would not want to be involved. She thought Cal had gone to Shannon's priest and asked him especially that she should be a bridesmaid, knowing that Phoebe liked and valued the girl, and he had given his permission.

Her father urged her forward and the people were turning around to look. She could see Cal and his foundry manager whose name she could in her panic not remember, the best man.

Phoebe stopped. As her father turned, still smiling, to encourage her and she could see the vicar at the front, she took her hand from through her father's arm. She turned around, pushed between Shannon and Margaret and then she staggered out of the church into the warmth of the May afternoon.

Just outside, she stopped. Her father had followed her out.

'Phoebe? Do you feel unwell?'

When she didn't answer he said, 'You're trembling. Is it just nerves? You can have a minute or two.'

Phoebe shook her head.

'I can't,' she said.

Her father went on looking at her.

'Are you ready to go back inside?'

'No.'

'Phoebe—'

'No.'

She walked away down the path, past the gravestones to the gate. He followed her.

'You must go back inside,' he said.

She turned and looked him in the eyes.

'No,' she said for the third time.

This time, she could see, he understood her. He did not ask any more, he walked back up the path and into the church.

Phoebe had no idea what to do now. She

stood, trying to decide and when she looked up Cal was standing there. He didn't look surprised, she thought.

'You've changed your mind,' he said.

Phoebe blinked. The sun was shining across the fields.

'I knew you had,' Cal said. 'I knew weeks ago.'

'I haven't.' She stumbled somehow over her tears. 'I tried to want this but I don't. I think … if you were honest you would say that you prefer Ailsa to me.'

Cal stared and Phoebe could tell that either this was not true or it had not occurred to him that such a thing could happen. Men, she thought, were so stupid. He looked amazed.

'That's what this is about?' He also, Phoebe thought, looked annoyed. And why should he not? 'Phoebe, the feelings that I had for Ailsa were gone the moment I knew she preferred my brother–'

'That's not true.' They were both taken aback at her vehemence, she could see. 'You always loved her. When you invite me over on Saturday nights it's as if I'm not there. Ailsa plays the piano and you listen and you like to talk about the same things and I might as well be at home for all the difference it makes. And – and I hate Chopin!'

'What?'

'You never shut up when she's there–'

'That's just a family thing. Ailsa's children are a continual pain in the side to me.'

'Of course they are. That's what families do. It's as though they're yours. You don't need your own children, you have Margaret and Luke and … and Danny.'

The words ran out and because she could not meet his gaze Phoebe screwed up her eyes against the sunshine. It was a perfect day for a wedding.

'I want somebody for myself,' Cal said, not quite shouting, and it was the first time she had seen him angry, 'not somebody who's belonged to someone else. Please, Phoebe, come back in with me. I'm so tired of being alone. I've wanted to marry you for so long–'

'But you aren't alone,' Phoebe said, 'that's half the trouble.'

'That's how it feels. Those other people, they all need me. I need you. Please.'

Phoebe didn't reply, didn't move. Cal was looking so hard at her that it almost hurt.

'Is there another reason?' he said.

'Perhaps.'

'What is it?'

'I realized that I didn't love you. I saw other

people in love, and I don't feel like that.'

Cal glanced back towards the church. He had accepted that it was no good, she thought.

'I see,' he said, finally and without looking at her. 'I'd better go back inside and tell them.'

Her mother was hovering in the doorway, Phoebe could see the pale green of her good costume. She came outside, tottering on heels she was unused to wearing.

'What on earth is going on?' she said. When Phoebe didn't immediately reply Cal said, 'There isn't going to be any wedding,' and he turned and was lost in the gloom of the church.

There were tears in her mother's eyes.

'Oh, Phoebe,' she said, 'what have you done?'

In the church the organist was valiantly playing hymns. The guests, embarrassed and almost bored, were whispering, heads down, as Cal walked up the aisle and then silence fell. The music stopped. He smiled at the vicar and told him what had happened and then he turned around and said to them, 'We're not going to have a wedding today. The party, however, will go ahead because in this time of rationing we have to make the best of everything and it has all been prepared. So why don't you make your way to my house and let's have a good time anyway.'

There was a minute or two of silence.

'Please,' Cal said, 'this is difficult for Phoebe and me. You can help by coming to the party.'

They began to get up. Some of them came to him, some of them walked slowly outside.

Luke and Danny waited until the church was empty and the two girls came back down the aisle towards them.

'Let's go to the beach,' Margaret said, pulling off the circle of flowers which Phoebe's mother had made as ornament.

They called by the house and put into a bag a picnic from the tables, which were full of food. Luke secreted cigarettes and a silver lighter, beer, glasses and a bottle of whisky and Margaret went upstairs to get towels and bathing suits and then they went.

They changed among the rocks, swam in the sea and the peace was wonderful away from the problems of the day. Shannon lay back in her borrowed swimsuit on her towel and thought guiltily of her father alone with the children. But then he wasn't expecting her back, had told her to have a good time and stay, so for once she saw no reason why she shouldn't.

She did feel bad for Phoebe but she did not want to be near. The grown-ups had caused the problem, as they nearly always did, so they could sort it out.

Later the boys dragged wood across the beach and lit a fire, they changed back into their clothes and sat, smoking and drinking and eating sausage rolls, and she thought it could not have been a better day if the wedding had gone ahead.

It was so companionable. They had gathered a lot of driftwood, some of it from the very top of the beach and from amongst the sand dunes so it was dry and burned well and some gave off sparks.

The darkness came in slowly.

'I should go,' she said. 'My dad doesn't like me to stay out in the dark, especially on Saturdays.'

'It's the drunks,' Danny said, 'and he should know.'

'Try not to hate him so much,' Shannon said.

'Oh,' Danny downed the last of his whisky,

'I don't hate him, I just think he's stupid and poor.'

'He is not stupid. Don't talk about him like that.'

'I'll talk about him any way I want. He's nothing to me. He's just a workman.'

Shannon knew it was only bitterness that made Danny say these things but she had to make herself not shout at him.

'What about Uncle Cal?' Luke said, laughing. 'He's had a bad day too. Poor bugger. Fancy wanting to marry an old stick like Miss Wilson. The whole thing's disgusting. People as old as that shouldn't be getting married.'

'He's been very kind to you and Miss Wilson's been good to me,' Shannon objected.

'You see the best in everybody,' Danny said. 'You'll make a wonderful nun.'

Shannon got up without another word and walked up the beach. It was a clear night and the sand was thick and cool beneath her feet.

She hadn't got to the top of the beach before Danny reached her. They walked, they didn't speak and when they got to the bottom of the hill below her house she stopped and said, 'I can go alone.'

'You mean he doesn't want to see me.'

'Don't pretend. You don't want to see him.'

'You're right,' Danny said. 'I never want to see him again as long as I live.'

Shannon went on up the hill without a backward glance.

It was quiet in her house. Her dad was lying on the settle, fast asleep. He heard her and moved and then got up and she sat down beside him and told him the day's events. He frowned when she had finished and she expected him to say, 'I don't understand. Miss Wilson loves bairns. You'd think she'd want to get married and Mr Gray is a good man and … he's respected and has plenty of money,' but he didn't.

They went to bed. It wasn't until Shannon was in bed that she looked up into the darkness and thought about Miss Wilson, pictured her with the baby in her arms and the bairns about her feet and how the fire was giving Miss Wilson's face a rosy glow, the flames lit her eyes.

Shannon said beneath her breath, 'Holy Mary,' as she had never done before, as she knew the truth.

Miss Wilson couldn't marry Mr Gray because she didn't want to and there was a very good reason for that. She loved the bairns and she loved the baby but the most important reason was that Miss Wilson had a thing about her dad. How awful.

Shannon couldn't sleep for thinking about it. Her dad obviously had no idea. She was sure that although he didn't talk about her mam, his head was full of her and that he missed her just as much now as he had done on the night she died.

Her dad had been with her mam since he was fifteen and he didn't think about other women like that. Poor Miss Wilson. How could she love a man like Shannon's dad?

Nobody could possibly care about him like that. He had four small bairns. He had no money and never would have and he had a number of very bad faults which nobody would ever cure him of. Her mam hadn't been able to, so what chance did anybody else stand?

Shannon let him off slightly here because her dad had always tried hard in spite of his drinking to be a good man. He just hadn't really managed it. She thought he had been a better father than many, though that wasn't saying much, but since her mam had died he had been brilliant with them all and had not been to the pub once.

He felt bad that she had to stay here with the children and in the evenings, now that it was light, he encouraged her to go out. She didn't go far. She often went to the church. She wished she could go now for the comfort. She prayed very hard but she didn't quite know for what.

Earlier that day but late enough for the visitors to have left, Ailsa followed Cal into the library.

'Are you all right?'

He looked at her.

'Of course you're not,' she said.

'I knew.'

'What?'

'I knew that Phoebe didn't want to marry me. I don't think she ever wanted to. I talked her into it. I thought she would come round.'

'I'm so sorry, Cal.'

'There's nothing anybody can do.' He sighed and then he said, 'It was my own fault. I can't think why I ever imagined in the first place that it would work. We had nothing in common. I think Phoebe only agreed because she was bored and lonely.'

'People have married for worse reasons,' Ailsa said.

'Do you think? I won't know now, will I?' he said lightly and he smiled at her and left the room.

Ailsa thought a lot about what had happened and the following day she went over to the vicarage. Phoebe's mother came to the door and ushered her inside. It was a lovely spring day beyond the windows.

Inside it smelled stuffy as though no one had noticed, as though no one had thought of sweeter air outside.

Mrs Wilson shut the door firmly behind Ailsa. Dust motes danced in what sunshine had made its way into the hall. Mrs Wilson led her into the drawing room and there Phoebe sat alone on the sofa. Her mother went out and left them.

'I just … wanted to see how you were after yesterday.'

'I'm fine, thank you. Do sit down.'

Ailsa perched on the edge of an armchair.

'I feel … I feel as though this is partly my fault, that you … that you blame me.'

Phoebe stared at her. 'How could I do that?'

'I'm in the way. I can see it now. I didn't intend anything. I was … lonely and I think I needed Cal to be there to help with the children and to take the responsibility and it wasn't right. It was very unfair. I think if Jaime hadn't died you and Cal would have been happily married by now. I'm going to find a house for us. I should have done it before and now I'm determined.'

'It wasn't like that, Ailsa,' Phoebe protested.

'Oh yes, it was. I expected too much. At least, I don't know what I expected, but I'm sure—'

'I think Cal loves you.'

It was Ailsa's turn to stare. 'Like I said, I'm in the way. Cal doesn't care about me, it's just that he feels he should be supportive. It shouldn't have come to this.'

'I don't love him,' Phoebe said.

Ailsa was already on her feet. 'He needs you,' she said, 'he's been there alone for so long.'

'Don't you care about him, Ailsa?'

'Not like that. I only ever loved Jaime,' and she hurried out.

The house was tiny. It would not have seemed so small if she had seen it straight after London. A middle terrace with two rooms downstairs, two up and—

'There's no bathroom,' Luke said, mooching around the upper storey.

'It's downstairs.'

He came in and stood in the middle of the back bedroom. It looked over the yards, the coal houses, the lavatories. The front room had a fireplace and looked across the street at other similar houses, a painting and decorating shop and the looming buildings of the steelworks.

'This is the best street in the town,' Ailsa said.

'And so near the works,' Luke said. 'Will I have to share a room?'

'Of course not. Margaret and I will share.'

'Dizzy heights,' Luke said and wandered down the stairs.

He was still growing, she thought, well over six foot tall. The house would seem even smaller to him.

Margaret had said nothing up to then. Now she turned with a decided look on her face. 'Why are we leaving Uncle Cal and Danny with Grandma?'

Put like that, Ailsa thought, it didn't sound too good. When she didn't reply Margaret said, 'Has Uncle Cal done something?' Margaret looked hard at her. 'He didn't have to marry Miss Wilson.'

That made Ailsa return the look. Margaret was so sharp these days.

'What do you mean?'

'He's rich. He can have anybody he wants.'

'It isn't like that–'

'It certainly is.'

'That's disgusting,' Ailsa said.

'No, it's common sense. Married to a man like Uncle Cal a woman could have everything, fur coats, decent jewellery, a nice car, a great big house and be bowed and scraped to in the butcher's. What more could anybody want?'

'Cynicism is not an attractive quality in somebody your age,' Ailsa said.

'That's why we're moving out, isn't it? So that Cal can marry somebody, but he won't. Having been able to have anybody he chose Miss Wilson. I can't think why but he's not going to marry her now.

'He won't take on a woman who turned him down so publicly. I don't know what she was thinking about. She leads the dullest life of anybody in the whole country.

'It would be much simpler if you married him. Then we could all stay together and not go traipsing around ghastly little houses pretending we're pleased.'

'That's ridiculous,' Ailsa said, flushing.

'Is it? It's not illegal, you know.'

'It just isn't done.'

'What a stupid phrase that is.'

'Margaret, you are very rude.'

And suddenly the adult in her daughter fell away and she was just a stubborn little girl, standing in the middle of the bare floorboarded room. She said, 'I don't want to go and leave Cal and Danny, so there,' and she ran away down the stairs.

Nineteen

The house was quiet when Keir came home. Could Shannon have taken all the children out with her? Usually she waited until he was there to go shopping because she couldn't cope with them all. He walked softly into the kitchen and there Phoebe knelt before the fire and before the tiny bath which Jessie had bought in better times. She had little Michael in the water and was sprinkling water on to him and he was looking up at her and smiling and she was talking nonsense to him, her voice gently animated.

She looked so much as Jessie had looked when they were first married and had Danny that Keir could hardly bear it. And then, just as he would have retreated, she saw him. Guilt hit her eyes. Crimson suffused her cheeks.

'Miss Wilson.'

'Mr Logan. Hello. I just … I came to see how Shannon was and she took the opportunity to collect Veronica from school and … I offered to bath the baby for her. He's so adorable.'

Adorable. Keir did not think it a word he had heard before, a posh word such as people like Miss Wilson used.

'You've got soap on your face,' he said.

'Oh. I was trying to keep it out of his eyes.'

She took the baby from the water and laid him on a towel on the hearthrug and patted him dry. She didn't look at Keir again.

'I'm sorry things didn't work out for you and Mr Gray,' he said.

'It was my fault,' she said, 'I think I was always meant to be an old maid.'

'He always liked Ailsa.'

Phoebe looked up then, her embarrassment gone.

'You're very astute.'

'No, I just have a long memory. As far as I can think she refused him because of his brother. A mistake.'

'I think she knew that, possibly almost from the beginning.'

'I sort of thought you might not marry him,' Keir said.

She looked surprised.

'Did you? Why was that?'

'Well, I don't know exactly, just that he had given you a ring and you had it on when you came to the house on Christmas night with Shannon after Jessie had died. And it looked so bright, so shiny and you wore it awkwardly like it wasn't meant to be there.'

'He'd asked me to marry him just before his brother was killed. Things were quite different and even then I didn't think he meant it.'

'And then you could have had him for breach of promise?'

'You think he might have thought so?'

Keir shrugged.

'Oh dear,' she said comically, 'and he was my last hope.'

'It cannot be that bad.'

She sighed, and a bit of hair escaped and slipped on to her cheek as she finished putting the baby into his nightwear and held him close against her.

'I'm thirty-five.'

'It didn't stop you from leaving him at the altar, though?'

'I'm more afraid of making a bad marriage than having a lonely life.'

'Are you now?' Keir said.

Her mother called out to Phoebe from the sewing room when she got back to the vicarage and Phoebe went gratefully in by the fire. The summer was finished and a long

305

summer it had been. People were supposed to be getting back to normal, whatever that was. Most of them had no idea of normality. Everything was altered.

The nights were drawing in and Phoebe had never felt as alone as she did now. That had prompted her to go and visit Shannon. She was glad she had done so. Shannon looked tired and Phoebe could see how grateful she was when Phoebe offered to take the baby so that she could go shopping and call at school. So there was not the conversation she had expected and needed but it was wonderful being there with the baby.

Phoebe went gratefully in by the fire. Her mother looked up from her sock-darning.

'Where's Daddy?' Phoebe asked.

'He went to visit the Slaters. Old Mr Slater is ill and asked for him. They've been friends for such a long time. Where have you been?'

'I went to see Shannon.'

'Oh, the dear girl. How is she?'

'I didn't see much of her.'

'An awful life she leads now with her dreadful father and all those children.'

'Yes. The Logan baby is just wonderful. He smells like warm fruit. I want to wrap him up and run out of the door with him,'

306

Phoebe said before she could stop herself. She saw the hunger in her mother's eyes. 'I'm so sorry. I feel like such a failure.'

Her mother put aside the basket of wool in her lap and she came over and said, 'It wasn't you, dearest, it was this dreadful war. It did such awful things to people. I miss my boys. I think if there had not been a war you would never have thought of marrying Callum. He wasn't right for you, I think I knew it from the beginning, but having lost our own boys we were so desperate to be grandparents and it isn't fair, it isn't right. Life is too precious to marry where one doesn't love. I'd rather you stayed right here with your boring old parents–'

'You aren't boring,' Phoebe said.

'Or did something else with your life, as I feel you must soon.'

Phoebe burst into tears. She told herself she was tired. Her mother stopped fussing and went to make her a cup of tea and after that made sure the conversation was general. But Phoebe went to bed and thought of nothing but Keir Logan and at last she admitted the truth to herself. She loved him. It was stupid.

She thought about how he had looked before she left him and about the house and the children and the baby and about his religion and his background. His parents had lived over on the coast, they were pit people and had come from Londonderry some time back and it was rumoured that his father had been in prison and his mother was a drunk.

Why did she have to want somebody like him? It could never come to anything. He would undoubtedly in time marry some other hapless female who liked him and would put up with his small army of children and she would be left here at the vicarage.

She saw herself as an old woman when her parents had died, forgotten, alone. She wished that she had gone through with her wedding, at least it would have been something, at least it would have been interesting and Cal was nice and his family were... Thinking of his family made her think of Ailsa and she revised her opinion. She could not bear to live in the same house as Ailsa.

Margaret came to visit shortly after this and Phoebe was glad of the company. Margaret sat down and started to tell her how her mother was insisting on them moving out of the house and how everything was awful.

Phoebe didn't know what to say. She was astonished.

'Why on earth does your mother want to move?' she said.

'She thinks she's in the way. I know she does, that if it hadn't been for her you and Uncle Cal would have got married and everything would have been all right.'

'It would never have been all right,' Phoebe said. 'We wouldn't have been happy, even if you had never come north. It was always … expedient.' What an awful word, like Cal was useful, accommodating, desperate. Perhaps he had been, perhaps they had both been.

'Would you come over and talk to her? Uncle Cal has gone to a meeting so he isn't there and I think she would like somebody to discuss it with.'

'I don't think I should.'

'Oh, please. She won't listen to me and…'

Another bad decision, Phoebe thought as she went back across the town with Margaret. Margaret deserted her as soon as they got inside. Ailsa and Cal's mother were sitting by the fire, not doing anything, but Ailsa did not look pleased to see her. She was polite, gave her tea, but Phoebe did not see that she could be of any use. Cal's mother was there so nothing could be said.

It was only when she felt she had stayed long enough and Mrs Gray had said very little that she tried to leave.

'I didn't realize Cal's mother was so angry with me. She barely spoke,' she said as the door closed and she and Ailsa were alone in the hall.

'Oh, don't worry about it,' Ailsa said, which Phoebe thought was generous of her.

'I wanted to say.' Phoebe stopped and turned to her, thinking if she didn't say it now there would always be bad feelings between them. 'It wasn't because of you. I mean I know we've never got on but it wasn't. It wasn't right.'

Ailsa's colour rose.

'I think it was partly my fault. I kept pretending that Cal was Jaime, it was easier whereas in fact they were never anything alike. I'm sorry things didn't work out.'

'Margaret says that you're leaving.'

'I have to.'

'Why?'

'Because if I don't I think Cal will ask me to marry him for all the wrong reasons and I would hate it. I don't think I was meant to be married. Jaime and I had an awful marriage.'

'I'm sorry. Perhaps neither of us is meant to be.'

'Perhaps not.' Ailsa, instead of opening the

big outside door, hesitated. 'Phoebe... You've got somebody else, haven't you?'

Phoebe was startled.

'No.'

'Yes, you have. I've seen people in love before and you have that look about you.'

'It isn't–'

'If it's something you really want–'

'It's not possible.'

'Is he married?'

'Not exactly.'

'What do you mean, "not exactly"?'

'His wife died. Oh dear, I wish I hadn't said that. It's awful to feel like that about somebody recently bereaved.'

'If war teaches you nothing else it teaches you that life must go on.'

'Perhaps you should remember it yourself,' Phoebe said, and she let herself out and strode away without giving Ailsa the chance to say anything more.

The following Saturday afternoon Ailsa went again to the little house, to try and convince herself that she could live there. She was standing in the front bedroom when she heard a noise downstairs, assumed it was one of the twins or more likely both of them and shouted down the stairs, 'I'm up here.'

Somebody took the stairs rapidly and Danny emerged from the gloom of the tiny hallway. Ailsa looked at him. He had been living with them since Christmas and it showed. He looked exactly as Jaime had looked when he was seventeen. It gave her a jolt. He had become one of them under their care. He was well dressed, confident, spoke almost as they spoke, was even charming on occasion, but he had Cal's decisiveness of mind, something which came from them working together, she imagined.

'I thought you and Cal were going pigeon shooting,' Ailsa said.

Since losing Phoebe, Cal was wont to take Danny with him when he went shooting or fishing. Luke hated killing things but Danny seemed content enough.

'He had to go back to the office.' Danny looked around. 'Are you really thinking of moving here?'

'I am, yes.'

She went into the other room. Outside it was raining and the smaller room was even darker than the other one.

'Why?'

'It's complicated.'

She walked back down the stairs and into the little back room whereupon Danny suggested brightly, 'I could move out instead. I could live here.'

Ailsa looked at him. His face was in shadow and half turned away.

'It isn't because of you,' she said.

Danny said nothing. He went into the front room. She followed him. There was a grubby brown carpet in there which made it look even worse.

'Did you hear what I said?'

'I heard you,' he said.

'But? This is not your fault.'

'You want to get away from me.' He looked directly at her such as Jaime never would have.

'No, I don't.'

'You must. You didn't ask me to come with you.'

'I didn't feel that I could. I didn't think you'd want to.'

'You could've asked me.'

'That would upset Cal.'

'Upset? He doesn't know yet, does he? He'll go mad. First Miss Wilson doesn't want him and now you want to walk out with half the household. I think it's something else.'

'What do you mean?'

Danny shifted, went to the window so that

he wouldn't have to look at her and from there he said, 'I think you don't want me near Margaret.'

'Oh, Danny, that's not true.'

'Isn't it?' He turned. 'It alters things you know completely when you find out you're that closely related to somebody. All the fancy you had for them dies away. I don't want to be the outsider all my life, Mrs Gray, I really don't.'

Up to then she hadn't thought Danny called her 'Mrs Gray'.

'I've lost my mam, my dad twice, that takes a bit of doing,' Danny said with a touch of humour, 'now I don't seem to be able to hang on to you or the twins either.'

'It's very complicated,' Ailsa said.

'Aye, it would be,' he said. 'I'm getting so as I even wish the old lady would be nice to me and that's keen.'

'I thought she was nice to you. You remind her of Jaime so much.'

'She kisses the twins. She never touches me. And you…'

'Me?'

'I remind you so much of your husband sometimes you hardly speak to me.'

Ailsa went to him, put her fingers into his hair and then she kissed him.

314

'Stop calling me "Mrs Gray",' she said, 'you can use my first name.'

'Can I come and live here with you, then?'

'It's too small. You're taller than Luke. What on earth would I do with the two of you, thumping up and down the stairs and taking up all the room? Besides, would you want to leave Cal?'

Danny looked at her.

'No,' he said, finally. 'No, I wouldn't.'

Phoebe's mother complained to her that she hadn't seen Shannon in weeks. 'Her father ought to let her out more often.'

'He's only there on Saturday afternoons and Sundays,' Phoebe said.

'Well then, why doesn't she bring the children with her?'

Phoebe looked doubtfully at her mother. 'They can be quite noisy.'

'I think noisy would be very nice,' her mother said. 'We could bake cakes, have a special party for them on a Saturday afternoon.'

Phoebe duly went to the Logan house and found Shannon exhausted, trying to look after the children, do the tidying up and see to her father's tea all at the same time. Phoebe took the baby from her and sat the

315

others around her and read a story while Shannon cooked.

'I mustn't stay,' she said eventually. 'Your father will be back soon.'

'He won't bite you,' Shannon said.

'I must go.' Phoebe got up and put the baby into his pram. He began to howl. 'You will come for tea on Saturday some time soon?'

'I would love to. What about my dad?'

'What?'

'He'll be on his own here and … I don't like leaving him. I know it sounds daft but you know what he's like, Phoebe, he'll go to the pub if there's nobody here.'

'I thought he didn't any more.'

Shannon looked knowingly at her. 'If he's left in the house with nothing to do and nobody to stop him … he can't be trusted.'

'Well, I suppose he could come as well,' Phoebe said.

When she had gone Shannon smiled to herself. She had thought a lot about this. Her dad was bound to find himself another woman some time, men always did, and even though he had small children somebody was bound to listen to his sweet Irish voice and let it get the better of her.

316

Miss Wilson really liked him and if there had to be another woman in the house Shannon would rather it was Phoebe than anybody else. She had the feeling that if she could get her dad together with Miss Wilson she would be able to free herself of the bairns, she might even be able to do the things that she wanted to do with her life. Whatever, it was worth a try, but she would have to talk her dad into going and that would take a lot of doing over the next few weeks.

The evening after she and Danny had looked at the little house Ailsa, feeling very defensive, walked into the study where Cal was working.

'I thought I'd better tell you before any of the children does. We're moving out.'

Cal didn't say anything.

'You've been very good to us, to the – to the detriment of–'

Cal got up from behind the desk.

'You're not seriously thinking about going?'

'We shouldn't have come here in the first place.'

'We are your family. Where else would you go?'

'I should have found a house, a job…'

She paused there but Cal just stood, looking at her so she went on, 'Anyway, I have got a house now.'

'Really?'

'Yes.'

'I see. Well, I hope it's a big house because I'm bloody well coming with you.'

'Don't be silly.'

'Do you really think I'll stay here with only my mother and Danny? Where is it?'

'Valley View.'

'Have you got a job?'

'Not yet.'

'You being so well qualified, of course. You can always go and play the piano in the Black Bull of an evening. That should suit you famously,' Cal said.

'I wouldn't do anything of the kind.'

'Of course you wouldn't, brought up so well as you were.'

His tone, for the first time that she could remember, was so unkind that Ailsa could not help remembering the horrid days of her childhood after her father had run off and left them. He had lived on in a town nearby for years but she had never seen him close to again.

All she had had was her music and her

mother, and her mother was always ill. She seemed to spend her time playing the piano to ease her mother's days. She rarely went to school when she was younger. Her mother could not be left.

She should have hated pianos. No wonder she had not played much all those years and she had thought it was Jaime's fault.

'You could always get a job at the Store.'

'The twins can get jobs. It's high time they did. Neither of them is doing anything at school. It won't hurt them to work.'

'Have you told them you want to leave?'

'I took them to the house.'

'And Danny?'

'Danny has seen it as well.'

'You'll have a good view of the steelworks from there. I don't know about the valley.'

Cal went back behind his desk and sat down. Ailsa didn't move.

'Was there something else? No? Then why don't you let me get on? I have a lot to do. Of course I won't have to work quite so hard after you've gone and left me with my mother and nine empty bedrooms. At least you won't be to keep.'

'Must you be so horrid?'

'No. Just think of me, when you're doling out sherbet lemons to snotty little kids and

319

I've got nobody for company but an old woman who like you preferred my brother to me.'

'Don't think I haven't regretted it,' Ailsa said. 'He drank, he neglected us, he was unfaithful to me–'

'If you went on like this I'm not bloody surprised,' Cal said. 'I'm well out of it. Go, for God's sake. Shut the bloody door after you.'

Ailsa ran out, slammed the door and went upstairs. She sat on the bed in her room and cried. She hadn't cried in such a long time. After a few moments the door clicked and Margaret tiptoed in.

'Mum?' she said, standing just inside the door.

'I'm fine.' Ailsa got up from the bed.

'We could hear you shouting from the hall.'

'You shouldn't have listened.'

'You and Daddy didn't row.'

'He was never there long enough,' Ailsa said and sat back down on the bed.

'I don't think I've ever heard Uncle Cal lose his temper before. He does actually sound just like Daddy, doesn't he? It's quite scary. Daddy was always losing his temper but you never shouted back at him like you do with Cal.'

Ailsa didn't go back downstairs and was rather surprised when it was very late and there was a knock on her door. Cal opened it.

Ailsa was in her nightdress and a thin dressing gown by then so she wouldn't have encouraged him inside, except that he came in before she said anything. He closed the door but didn't advance into the room, just stood.

'I'm sorry. It's nothing to do with me what you do. I don't seem able to...' he said and then stopped. 'I know why you don't like me–'

'Cal–'

'I know it isn't anything personal and I know I'm nothing like him, but to you there is enough of him in me to make you dislike me.'

'I don't dislike you.'

'Yes, you do. You must – you must go if you want to. I even think it's probably a very good thing, that if you were alone you might find somebody who isn't anything like Jaime, somebody that you could...'

'He treated me very badly,' Ailsa said.

'Yes, I know he did.'

'He was … he used to hit me when he was angry. I thought it was my fault.'

She hadn't ever said the words before, had never acknowledged them to herself.

'How could it be?'

'Oh yes, it could. After somebody's hit you, you don't want them any more. I didn't want to go to bed with him.'

Ailsa was surprised as the tears slid down unaided, unheeded. She was, she decided, so tired of crying, she was not going to do it again.

'Or anybody else,' he said in to the silence. And she nodded and used the heel of her hand to dry her face briskly.

'You think I'm going to hit you?'

'No.'

'But when Phoebe was there between us you felt safe?'

'Yes, I suppose.'

'I do understand, but you know, men aren't all like that.'

'I know that in my head but…'

Cal nodded.

'I will help you move. You can even take some of the more hideous pieces of furniture which I shall persuade my mother she needs to get rid of. I'm sorry I shouted at you. I don't know why I didn't realize from the beginning.'

'How could you?'

'How could you not keep secrets from me considering who I am? Tomorrow we'll sort out what you need and I will do everything I can to help and I will make you a proper income–'

'That's not right–'

'Yes, it is. People will only talk if you have to get some awful job and you'll hate me. Jaime was entitled to half the foundry. We'll talk about it tomorrow. Try not to be upset. It's over now.'

In the shadows on the landing Margaret waited, holding her breath, until Cal went down the stairs and then she turned to the two boys who were even further in the darkest shadows against the wall.

'Holy shit,' she said.

Luke was turned away.

'Luke?'

'How could Dad do that to her? How could he? She's so little, so … I'm glad he died!'

'Don't say that.'

'I am,' Luke said and he wrenched away from her restraining hand, got up and left Danny and Margaret sitting there in the warm gloom on the late autumn night.

'I'm staying here with him,' Danny said.

'I don't want to go anywhere.'

'You have to.'

Margaret nodded and then they both got up and followed Luke into his bedroom. He was hanging out of the window into the night.

'I can hear the sea.'

'It doesn't mean you're going to be like Dad, either of you,' Margaret said, including Danny in her gaze.

'You really think not?' Luke said.

'What's really worrying,' said Margaret, also hanging out the window and sniffing the salty air, 'is that if Danny isn't careful he could turn into Uncle Cal.'

'Oh bugger,' Danny said.

Cal was right, Ailsa thought. The window from the dining room and back yard looked out into the big shop which Cal had built on the old railway line to house the expansion of the works just before the war. It was a white building and you couldn't see around or past it.

From upstairs you could, if you tried hard, see the way that the moors gave way to fields. It was the wrong way to see the sea. It was the wrong way to see anything but somehow for all its lack of space her heart did not fail her when she viewed her little kingdom.

It was the first house that she had ever chosen for herself and she liked it. She liked the idea of neighbours, she liked the way that other people lived across the narrow street, she loved the yard behind it and the back lane and the sounds of the foundry which could be heard throughout the day. She felt safe here, knowing that Danny and Cal were at work just beyond. It felt right.

She liked the little fireplace in the bedroom, a black half moon which she was convinced one day she would light. She liked the way that the twins did not object and how Cal gave her exactly the right pieces of furniture. She liked the way his mother came down the steps from the dining room into the kitchen and said, 'Oh, Ailsa, you'll get all the sun in here.'

Ailsa had kissed her and she had looked surprised and pleased, and even more pleased when Ailsa said, 'You must come and see us often.'

'Oh, I shall. Look at how good the oak table is in here,' and she went back and smoothed her hands on its top beneath the window.

It did look wonderful, Ailsa thought, following her. The sun shone down on the back yard and Ailsa felt at peace for the first time in years.

Twenty

Keir had gazed around him when he went to tea with Phoebe's parents that autumn.

'Do you like the place, Mr Logan?' Phoebe asked shyly.

The children were seated on rugs on the lawn. It was a beautiful day, just like summer. Shannon was talking to Mrs Wilson. Mr Wilson was playing a ball game with Mary and Veronica and they were laughing and shouting and he was smiling.

Mrs Wilson held the baby and little Theresa was sitting against Shannon, holding with fascination an old doll which Mrs Wilson had found in the attic, claiming it had belonged to Phoebe when she was a little girl.

'It's like a dream,' he said, 'like a whole family.'

'Yes. I have one end of it and you have the other. You don't talk about your own parents.'

Keir didn't know what to say but since Phoebe went on looking enquiringly at him he began.

'We left Derry when I was small. My father came from a good family. My mother didn't. His parents cast him off when he married her because she was Catholic and poor and he was Protestant and rich. He didn't know how to work, he hated being poor. In the end he ran away, left us. She liked the bottle too much.'

'And she died?'

'She fell down the stairs drunk. I was ten. I met Jessie later and things got better. I wanted to be a good parent.' He laughed. 'Look at me.'

'I think you are a good parent.'

'You haven't seen me drunk.'

'I thought you'd stopped.'

'Drunks never stop. Mind you, I sing well when I'm drunk.'

Phoebe laughed. Keir gazed across at the trees, where the leaves had turned orange and brown.

'I can't forgive myself for Danny or for treating Jessie like I did over it.'

'It wasn't right,' Phoebe said, 'but it was understandable, surely? You aren't very good at forgiving yourself.'

'Or other people.'

They strolled down the gardens. Where it wasn't cultivated it had woodland and a stream at the bottom. There was a big area for the hens, an orchard and a summer-house placed so that it looked clear across the valley. The door was open. Keir stepped inside. Phoebe went inside too.

To his delight the whole thing turned around into the shade.

'Why, it's wonderful,' he said.

'Isn't it? We used to spend hours playing in here when the boys were small.'

'You miss them a lot, eh?'

'They were both much cleverer than me. Edward was going to be a doctor and Francis a solicitor.'

'I think you're very clever,' Keir said, sitting back on the cushions which covered the wicker seat he was sitting on.

'Do you?' She looked surprised, pleased.

The pale sunshine was flooding in and turning Phoebe's hair into a shiny curtain and Keir had to stop himself from wanting to touch her. It was his turn to be surprised. He was ashamed too. Jessie was dead. What was he doing? He wanted to get up and walk away but Miss Wilson would think him very rude and she had been so kind. She would also think he was an upstart. She had left the most eligible man in the area at the altar. What would she want with a drunken, ignorant workman?

He was glad he hadn't left within seconds because Phoebe bestowed upon him such a sweet smile as he thought he had never seen.

'Yes, I do,' he said. 'You call Michael "adorable".'

'He is adorable.'

Keir wanted to say, 'So are you,' but he didn't, he just went on looking at her as Phoebe smiled into his eyes.

If ever a woman should get married and have children it was Phoebe Wilson. He couldn't understand why she hadn't married Mr Gray.

Nobody said anything much after that but Keir recognized the feeling of happiness, the first time since long before Jessie had died. The first time, he thought with shame, since he had discovered that Danny was not his son. He missed Danny almost as much as he missed her but sitting in the summerhouse with Phoebe was like a plaster on a cut finger. It was not much but it was a little light in the darkness of his feelings.

When tea was over Mr Wilson, not knowing quite what to do with his unwelcome guest, mischievously invited him into the library.

'Do you read much?' he said.

Keir smiled. 'My passions so far have been my wife and the bottle, as I'm sure you know. It hasn't left much over for literature.'

'You must have a favourite author?'

'I'm very fond of James Joyce,' Keir said with a grin and Mr Wilson could not help but smile.

When it was late and they had gone Mr Wilson sipped at his nightly glass of whisky and said to his wife, 'That man has lovely children.'

She looked at him.

'Do you think so?' she said.

'Don't you?'

'Oh yes, I thoroughly enjoyed them but I think most women feel like that. This is such a big house. Sometimes it echoes with silence somehow. Len...' she said and stopped.

'What?'

His wife didn't go on. Her colour rose, faded, her breathing altered and she looked at the door as though Phoebe, who had gone to bed half an hour ago, was about to walk in.

'You don't think Phoebe has feelings for this man, do you?'

He stared at her and then into his glass.

'Surely not,' he said.

'I think she may. I think he is the reason she didn't marry Callum.'

'Good God,' Mr Wilson said. 'And we invited him here as though we were friends.'

His wife didn't say anything.

'Do you think that's possible?' he said. 'It would be ridiculous.'

'I don't think he's aware of it, if that's any comfort.'

'Just as well. Phoebe is our only child. She will be very well off one day.'

Mrs Wilson nodded and then said, 'Well off and alone?'

'That's not going to happen. Another man will come along–'

'Len, she's thirty-five and she quite obviously doesn't want another man. If she can't have the one she wants I think Phoebe will never marry.'

'She couldn't marry him.'

'Wouldn't it be worse if she grew old and didn't have him when she's so very much in love, no matter what he's like? Life is supposed to go on. What else are we here for? And you and I … we've lost our sons and we have no grandchildren, nothing to look forward to.'

'But a man like that, uneducated and…'

'I've seen worse and so have you. He works

hard and he seems to be doing his best. Shannon is a lovely girl and it was so nice to hear the sound of children in our house again.'

'Oh my dear,' he said, and he went over and kissed her.

Having got the children to bed Shannon gave the baby to her father as they sat over the kitchen fire and she said, 'You've been very quiet since you got back.'

'I'm tired. It was a hard week.'

'Mr and Mrs Wilson have a lovely house. What did you think of the library?'

'It's very fine,' he said.

'And Miss Wilson?'

'What?'

Shannon ignored the look in his eyes. Really, she thought, men were hopeless.

'Do you like Miss Wilson?'

'She's all right. I don't know her very well. She's good to you. She likes Michael.'

'She likes all the children. She's very kind. Don't you think she's bonny?'

'No, I think she looks washed out,' he said. 'It isn't natural living like that with her parents.'

'There are some things you can't help,' Shannon said.

'She could have married Cal Gray.'

'You can't marry just anybody and expect to be happy.'

'No, indeed. This bairn's asleep. I think I'll take him up and go to bed.'

Shannon took a deep breath before he got up. There was nothing to lose here.

'Miss Wilson fancies you.'

Keir looked at her and the look told Shannon she could have waited a hundred years before her dad came to the same conclusion.

'What on earth makes you think so?' he said.

'She does. I can tell.'

'A woman like that?'

'Why wouldn't she?'

'Well, because she's who she is. She likes the bairns and she likes your company and you shouldn't go around saying things like that. I never heard anything so daft,' and he took Michael and was away up the stairs before Shannon could think of anything else to say.

Keir could not rid his mind of the image of Phoebe and how much she liked his children and how kind she had been to him. Several times in the days that followed he came home to find her in his kitchen. He came to play games with his mind on the way back up the hill from the town, wondering whether she would be there, and it was caught up in how Jessie had always been there. And on the days that Phoebe was not he could feel his mood swing down as he walked into the house.

He never betrayed it to Shannon because it wasn't fair. In a way he came to hope that Phoebe wouldn't be there, because his life was turning once again into the upswings and downswings that sent him to the beer. He could hardly bear it.

And Shannon was right, Miss Wilson cared about him. How had he not been able to see it? It was not the way that she blushed, plenty of shy women did the same. It was the way that she looked at his child, how tender she was with the little ones and how her name was always on their lips. They talked constantly of her and of the games she had played with them.

Many a time that autumn he would get home and they were just coming back from the walks on the beach or in the town. They all benefited and he thought his children were lucky, they had had a good mother and now they had Phoebe, at least for a little time.

He treasured the way that the worry went from Shannon's eyes and it was because of Phoebe. She didn't come at weekends when he was there and he understood. But it made him long for the weekdays, he grew to miss her so much.

In the end therefore as the autumn turned into winter he took all the courage he had and went up to the old vicarage late on Saturday afternoon when Shannon had told him that Phoebe and her mother were going into Sunderland to see relatives.

She had been right. Mr Wilson was alone. He didn't look all that pleased. Keir thought that the Wilsons knew very well which way the wind was blowing and were unhappy about it, and wished they had not invited him and his family into their home. So it was with a struggle that Keir allowed himself to be taken into the library and to be reminded of his favourite day that autumn, when they had picnicked on the lawn like a real family with three generations and not as they were, the Wilsons without their sons and he without his parents.

Mr Wilson turned to him, hard-eyed.

'What can I do for you, Mr Logan?' he said.

Keir's heart gave. His ready tongue

deserted him.

'I just wanted to talk to you. Miss Wilson has … has taken to spending a great deal of time at my house.'

'I'm aware of it and I'm very sorry for it. Unfortunately she is too old to be taken aside and told that it will not do. I wish in so many ways that we had not asked you here.'

'You regret it? I'm sorry.' His precious afternoon cracked like old china in his memory under Mr Wilson's dismissive gaze. 'The thing is–'

He got no further, though whether he would have been able to say anything more was in doubt.

'That you imagine I should entrust my daughter's future to you?' Mr Wilson said.

Mr Wilson didn't go on though Keir gave him plenty of time. As he did so he remembered the day his father had left and he realized then that what had hurt him most about Danny was that their fathers had done the same kind of thing. And even then, he thought, you bastard, you couldn't look after him. The worse side of his nature told him that Danny had done just fine without him, and it was true, but he thought there might never be a good word between them again this side of purgatory.

'Is it my lineage you don't care for?' he said. 'Because I can tell you now that my father was a rich man's son. They had an estate in Londonderry.'

Mr Wilson looked sceptically at him.

'You think I'm making it up? My mother was a kitchen maid in the house. I know, it's like one of the old fairy stories, only it didn't have a happy ending. I doubt things like that ever do. They learned to hate one another and when the quarrels and the drink extinguished what was left he walked out.

'She was a fallen Catholic, she'd married a Protestant and there's nowhere you can do that and be accepted to either side.'

The room was silent for so long that he finally said, 'I'm not going to – to address Miss Wilson without your permission and I haven't said anything to her so you've nothing to worry about. I'm sure you're right. It's not an ideal situation for a deli-cately brought up young woman.

'I know I wouldn't have me.' He smiled at that and Mr Wilson nodded in under-standing. 'Four small children and a house at Lane End. It's not the stuff that dreams are made on. I'm just trying to be honest here. Perhaps you could stop her from coming to my house. I think my neighbours are starting to talk and she at least has a reputation to lose,' and he went home.

Mrs Wilson duly came home. As soon as she could she took her husband aside and said, 'What has happened?'

Mr Wilson tried to pretend but they had been married too long for him to be able to deceive her, so in the end he told her what had happened.

'And are you going to tell Phoebe that she shouldn't go there any more?'

'Hardly,' he said. 'What do you suggest?'

'I think you should tell her the man wants to marry her.'

'I cannot do that.'

'You don't think she's old enough at thirty-five to decide her own life? He could have gone behind your back and asked her himself or worse, he could have made up to her. They're adults, Len, we aren't talking about fifteen-year-olds. He did you the courtesy–'

'Do you really want Phoebe to end up in Lane End with a man like that and half a dozen children?'

'No, I don't, no more than I want to see her here, frustrated and lonely. There is an alternative, of course.'

He looked at her. She had obviously given this thought.

'And what is that?'

'They could all come and live here.'

'That's a ridiculous suggestion.'

'Is it? The best day we had this autumn was when the Logans were here. Dear God, I've become so bored. Haven't you?'

'He's a – a Catholic.'

'Does he go to church?'

'Strangely enough,' her husband said caustically, 'I didn't ask him.'

Phoebe was in her bedroom when she heard her father call up the stairs.

'Can you come down a minute?' he said. When she did so she found both her parents standing in the library and for a moment it was like the day the telegram came when Francis had been killed. Phoebe's heart beat so hard it almost hurt.

'What's wrong?' she said.

'Nothing,' her mother said.

Her father looked hard at her.

'Mr Logan came to see me this afternoon.'

'It's not one of the children, or Shannon?'

'No, no. Nothing like that. He wants to marry you.'

Phoebe heard the words echo several

times over. She had never fainted in her life but she thought she might now.

'He said that?'

'Yes, he did.'

'But he's given no indication—'

'He told me that he wouldn't say anything to you if your mother and I were set against it.'

Phoebe wanted to turn and run out of the house, across the town and up the hill to Lane End, but she stood there and said only, 'And are you?'

It was her mother who put in, 'Do you want him, Phoebe?'

'Oh yes,' she said, 'yes, I do.'

And her father said, 'You could love a man like him?'

'I don't know what he's like. I don't know what other men are like. I only know that he's the only man I've ever felt this way about. I'm sorry, I know how disappointed you were when I didn't marry Cal but I couldn't. It would have been wrong in every way. I don't want to upset you when you've had so much to bear—'

'Phoebe, if he's what you want then you must marry him,' her mother said. She looked at her father and he said,

'We think, if Mr Logan is agreeable, that

341

you should be married and that you should live here.'

Phoebe burst into tears.

It was mid-evening by the time Phoebe reached Lane End and she thought it was possibly the most beautiful evening which had ever graced the earth, even though it was freezing cold with a wind which came off the sea.

She went down the row and banged on the door and Keir opened it, as she knew he might, Shannon being busy with the other children at that time of night. He had a child on each hip, and when they saw Phoebe they squealed to be down and when he let them they ran to her.

Phoebe talked to them, went inside and then said shyly, 'I'd like to speak to you.'

Shannon came over.

'I'll take the bairns. Here, Dad, your jacket,' and she pushed them out of the door.

Nobody spoke. They walked down the hill and across the little bridge which housed the fishing boats and down the narrow street towards the harbour and past what she knew was his favourite pub and further on. Darkness had set in long since. Lights burned in the houses behind them. Keir leaned against the rail and looked out to sea.

'Your father told you I came to him? He thought it was a spectacular piece of cheek. I wish you'd seen his face. I don't know what I was thinking of. I'm sorry. My wife is dead and just like every other stupid bugger on the planet I'm trying to replace her and I know you like me. I know that seems very vain considering I have nothing to give you or any woman–'

'I love you.'

There was silence. He turned.

'Miss Wilson–'

'I think you ought to call me "Phoebe", don't you?'

'Should I?' He paused there and then he said, 'Phoebe… Holy Mary, Mother of God. Is this a good idea?'

'What?'

'If you … if you feel inclined to smack me over the face for this you do but … it seems to me that you like my children and … could you, would you… Phoebe?'

She laughed. She said, 'I never heard my name so beautifully said. Is that God's voice behind you?'

'Ah, you're making fun of me now. I want you to be my wife. Would you take on a poor Irish sinner?'

'I might,' she said with a smile in her voice.

'And what about your parents?'

'They've lost everything they hold dear except me.'

'If they hold you dear they'll let you go.'

'And haven't you got the Irish tongue on you, Keir Logan?'

He caught her to him and kissed her and somehow in the process they both dropped ten years and it was all merry.

'The only thing is,' Phoebe said, as they walked back up the hill to tell Shannon and the children, 'that I think my parents would like me to be married in the parish church. Do you think you could do that?'

'I think it would redress the balance,' he said.

Cal sent Ailsa a piano. It was not the baby grand from his house, it would not have fit into the tiny rooms of the terraced house which was hers, but she opened the door one morning not long after she had moved to find four men and the prettiest upright that she could remember. It was old fashioned and had holders for where the candles should go and some lovely kind of inlaid wood which she did not recognize.

'Where would you like this, Mrs Gray?' one of the men asked.

Ailsa stared.

'Oh,' she said and then, 'you'd better bring it in.'

'Aye, that was the idea,' he said and grinned.

Half an hour later, when they had negotiated the hall and settled it in her dining room on the back wall and they had gone, there was another knock on her front door. It was the piano tuner.

'Don't tell me,' she said, 'Mr Gray sent you.'

'Pianos need tuning after they're moved,' he said and came in.

When he had gone Ailsa sat down and played it for an hour or so. Then she walked over the road and through the cutting which led into the foundry and along the narrow passageway which led to Cal's office.

Nobody announced her. She walked through the shadows which the various shops cast across the smaller building where the paperwork was done and the decisions made, and his door was open. He was sitting at the desk and didn't look up, thinking, no doubt, that it was just another problem from somewhere in the works. When he did look up she could see he was ready to deal with it.

'You look tired,' she said and then she went behind the desk and kissed him briefly on the lips. 'Thank you for my piano. It's beautiful.'

'I thought you might like it.'

'Who'll play the piano at your house?'

'I'm going to take lessons,' he said.

'Liar. Cal?'

'Mm?'

'What are you doing on Saturday night?'

'Nothing.'

'If you come over to my house I could play for you.'

'That would be lovely,' he said.

'Will you bring a bottle of wine?'

'I'll bring champagne.'

'I'll make dinner.'

Danny was hard at work when his father stopped by. Would he never stop thinking of Keir as his father, he thought impatiently. Keir stood in the doorway of his small office. It was mid-afternoon and his work was over. His face was dusty, he had been there since very early morning.

'Could I have a word?'

'I suppose so, though Mr Gray deals with everything–'

'It's not about work. Can I come in?'

'Shut the door,' Danny offered, sitting back in his chair and trying not to care.

'I just don't want you to find out from anybody else. You think badly enough of me anyway and rightly so. I'm getting married.'

'Married? Who on earth would marry you?' Danny said, unable to stop himself.

'Miss Wilson.'

Danny looked into Keir's dark eyes.

'Miss Wilson is marrying you?'

'Yes. Not just yet, though. I know you think your mother–'

'No, I don't think it,' Danny said swiftly. 'She was always too good for you and Miss Wilson will always be too good for you, but if you have to marry somebody I'd rather Miss Wilson than anybody else. She's nice.'

'You think so?'

'Oh aye.'

Keir was smiling.

'I want you to be my best man,' he said. 'I know you think–'

'You don't know what I think,' Danny said, 'your bloody trouble is that you've never known what anybody thinks.'

'We're being married in the parish church in the spring. Will you do it? I need the support.'

'Ah, you're bloody hopeless,' Danny said.

Keir was smiling now.

'We're going to go and live with her parents. I'm coming up in the world.'

'Well, there was only one direction for you to go,' Danny said.

'Will you do it?' his dad said, 'Shannon and Margaret can be bridesmaids–'

'Oh, not again. Remember what happened last time?'

'It isn't going to be like that,' Keir said, 'it's going to be nothing like that, Danny Boy.'

'All right, then.'

Keir paused.

'Will you come for tea some time? You do remember where we live?'

And he left. Danny sat, staring at the closed door and remembering his dad singing to him on the beach and how it was the best thing ever and the best thing ever was never lost, was caught there for all time.

Keir had been a good dad to him for sixteen years and possibly he would be a good dad again for the next sixteen. It was not biology, he thought, which determined such things. It was not secrets. It was all down to whether people cared for one another and there was very little you could do about that. Keir had always been his dad and always would be. There was no justice in life. His mam was dead, and Jaime Gray.

There was a knock on the door and when he spoke Cal opened it.

'Your dad was here. Is everything all right?'

Oh dear, Danny thought, another complication. There was no point in putting it off.

'He came to tell me that he's marrying Miss Wilson.'

Cal didn't say anything. Danny didn't blame him but after he got over the shock he smiled and said, 'That's nice. Can you come into the works? I want to show you something.'

Danny got up from behind the desk. He loved to hear Cal say that. He got up and followed him and he thought, this is where I should be, among the castings and the heat and the men and the work. I was born for this. It's mine. It's where I should be.

The publishers hope that this book has given you enjoyable reading. Large Print Books are especially designed to be as easy to see and hold as possible. If you wish a complete list of our books please ask at your local library or write directly to:

Magna Large Print Books
Magna House, Long Preston,
Skipton, North Yorkshire.
BD23 4ND

This Large Print Book, for people
who cannot read normal print,
is published under the auspices of

THE ULVERSCROFT FOUNDATION